James Campbell was born in Inverness. During the war he flew on thirty-eight bombing operations with No. 158 Halifax Squadron based at Lisset, Yorkshire. After the war he returned to journalism, turning down the chance of continuing in the RAF on a short service commission. For the last twenty-two years he has been the Lobby Correspondent of a daily newspaper. In 1962 he was the only journalist to anticipate Selwyn Lloyd's 'lollipop' Budget, and Granada TV's 'What the Papers Say' acclaimed his story as 'the scoop of the year'.

Also by James Campbell

MAXIMUM EFFORT

James Campbell

The Bombing of Nuremberg

Futura Publications Limited

A Futura Book

First published in Great Britain in 1973
by Allison & Busby Limited

First Futura Publications edition 1974
Reprinted 1977

ISBN 0 8600 7063 8

Printed in Great Britain by
Cox & Wyman Ltd,
London, Reading and Fakenham

Futura Publications Limited
110 Warner Road, Camberwell, London S.E.5.

To the dead fliers of R.A.F. Bomber Command and the German Night-Fighter Force, and to the memory of my mother Elizabeth Ann Campbell.

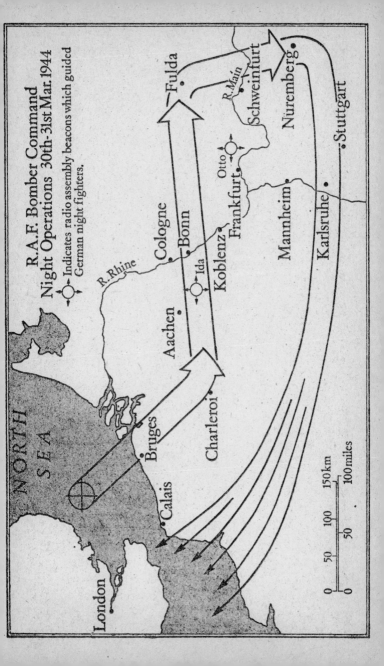

R.A.F. Bomber Command
Night Operations 30th–31st Mar. 1944

⊕ Indicates radio assembly beacons which guided German night fighters.

NORTH SEA

London

Calais
Bruges
Charleroi
Aachen
Cologne
Bonn
Ida
Koblenz
Frankfurt
Otto
R. Rhine
R. Main
Fulda
Schweinfurt
Nüremberg
Mannheim
Karlsruhe
Stuttgart

0   50   100   150km
0   50   100 miles

Acknowledgements

This book could not have come into being without the co-operation and wholehearted assistance of those whose experiences of the Nuremberg raid are related in it. They are too numerous to list here, but their names appear in the book – and I am most grateful to them all.

I owe a debt of special gratitude to Marshal of the Royal Air Force Sir Arthur Harris, who was kind enough to allow me to interview him, and to the late Air Marshal Sir Robert Saundby who, as Deputy Commander-in-Chief of wartime Bomber Command, was Sir Arthur's right-hand man and whose help was of the greatest value in compiling this work. My thanks, also, to Air Chief Marshal The Honourable Sir Ralph Cochrane, who was Air Officer Commanding No. 5 Bomber Group, and to Air Vice-Marshal D. C. T. Bennett, who was Air Officer Commanding Pathfinder Group.

And I am indebted to Herr Hans Ring of the Gemeinschaft der Jagdflieger E.V. in Munich, whose assistance in tracing German night-fighter crews was as invaluable as other researches he so unselfishly made.

Also highly appreciated is the help given by Air Vice-Marshal S. W. B. Menaul, s.a.s.o., Bomber Command Headquarters; Wing Commander Pat Daniels, Pathfinder leader on the Nuremberg raid; the R.A.F. and Luftwaffe aircrews for their accounts of the action and the records they sent; Oberst im Generalstab Johannes Janke of Munich; the Air Ministry Historical Branch; Mr. Thomas Cochrane, deputy chief information officer; Mr. David Irving, author of *The Destruction of Dresden*, who passed on to me material he possessed on the Nuremberg raid; the official historians responsible for *The Royal Air Force, 1939-1945*; Mr. George Clark, deputy lobby correspondent of *The Times*, for translating some of the many German documents and communications; and Mr. Irving Farren.

JAMES CAMPBELL

Chapter One

Low, heavy cloud hung over the Pathfinder airfield at Wyton, near Huntingdon, as it began to stir to life on the morning of 30th March 1944. Not a portent of best possible flying conditions – but the weather, paradoxically, was no deterrent to the type of mission flown from this field. Indeed, even as the blackout shutters were being lifted from the windows of the station's communications room the teleprinter made an early start by clicking out the code-name Tampa. Bomber Command Headquarters were calling on Meteorological Flight 1409 for yet another arduous and dangerous sortie into enemy territory in broad daylight; and this time it was a special report on weather conditions over Germany itself, particularly in respect of the southern part of the country, that was urgently required.

The duty aircrew – Flying Officer T. Oakes and Flight Lieutenant R. G. Dale – had just finished breakfast when they were summoned to the briefing room. While they were receiving their orders, out on the tarmac a sleepy-eyed ground-crew clambered over a Mosquito – capable of a high speed, but in this case unarmed – making a last-minute pre-flight check. Whatever the destination, there would be a lone, nerve-racking deep-penetration flight into hostile skies ahead for the Mosquito's two-man crew and nothing could be left to chance. But neither Oakes nor Dale seemed especially concerned when they eventually hurried out to the plane, climbed into the cramped cockpit and ran through the customary take-off drill. They were both experienced Met fliers, and they looked upon their assignment as just another job.

Within minutes, the Mosquito's powerful in-line Merlin engines thundered into life with the harsh, crackling, staccato note peculiar to them. From the control tower a green Aldis lamp flashed. And then the plane streaked arrow-straight down the runway and was airborne, to be lost to the view of the few watchers below almost at once as it sliced into the cloud base.

It may on the surface have been just another job to Oakes and Dale, but as they set course for the enemy coast they were nevertheless in no doubt of the importance of their mission. They knew that the planning of any air raid depended primarily on an anticipation of the weather conditions likely to prevail not only over the proposed target area at the crucial time but also over the home bases of the returning bombers. And they also knew that on this occasion they would be the main source of information upon which forecasts could be made.

Accurate forecasting of the weather was a hit-and-miss business at the best of times – even in peacetime, when meteorologists had at their disposal the latest reports from Atlantic weather-ships to use in conjunction with the pooled data from weather-stations throughout Europe. But now, with Atlantic shipping having to maintain strict radio silence and with Europe occupied, information was at a minimum and huge uncharted areas regularly appeared on the Royal Air Force's daily weather charts, taxing the skill of forecasters beyond reasonable expectation. Met flights over the Atlantic and the North Sea were therefore crucial to the planning of air operations in the European theatre of war, and they had to be carried out daily in even the most adverse conditions.

Much, then, depended on the observations of Oakes and Dale. During their unescorted flight they would note, among other things, the amount and height of cloud and the direction and speed of the wind—vital factors in the timing of a large-scale raid; and they would also judge where vapour trails would be most likely to form, knowing that it was this phenomenon that betrayed to the Germans the presence of high-flying bombers on clear nights.

Air Ministry records show that the Mosquito flew as far as Aachen, though comparable German sources indicate that it penetrated as far south as Leipzig. Be that as it may, the information its crew brought back formed the basis of the first weather report of the day to Bomber Command Headquarters.

But the actual report was not the responsibility of Oakes and Dale. Immediately after their return, Bomber Command's senior Met officers throughout the bomber groups had held a conference by means of the 'scrambler' telephone to evaluate the data they had provided.

Like the fliers, these officers were always acutely aware of how much depended on the accuracy of their judgments and they preferred to err on the side of caution rather than risk placing aircrews in jeopardy – although the ifs and buts with which they usually punctuated their briefings did nothing to endear them to bomber crews who only too often encountered weather that was totally different from that which had been forecast.

In this instance, there had been no less caution than was customary. For the most part, said the Met men, the night would be suitable for operations from all bases: but they added a warning that there would be the risk of local industrial-smoke troubles in Command Groups 4 and 6, with valley fog towards dawn. For the outward flight it was predicted that there would be broken cloud everywhere except in Southern Germany, where cloud was expected to be layered. Over Nuremberg there would be strata cumulus to 8000 feet, with patchy cloud at 15,000 to 16,000 feet; and it was thought, too, that there was the likelihood of a crescent moon appearing.

German Meteorological Service records show that, in fact, on the afternoon of 30th March 1944 – and for most of the evening – the weather over Nuremberg was cloudy with a light wind. In the early evening the cloud ceiling lifted from 600 feet to 3000 feet, but mist later brought visibility down to little over a mile.

At his headquarters in a wood outside High Wycombe, Buckinghamshire, the Commander-in-Chief Bomber Command sat at his desk and pondered on the Met reports before him. Sir Arthur Harris – 'Bert' to his friends, 'Bomber' to the public, and 'Butch' to his aircrews—had been a major in the Royal Flying Corps during World War I and had led a squadron of fighters, based in England, whose task it had been to bring down German zeppelins: so he was no mere armchair warrior. He was generally acknowledged to be a grim man who could freeze an Eskimo with a look; a man of explosive temperament; a man of few words – all of them forceful. Bulky in frame, his grey eyes staring coldly over the half-moon glasses perched on the end of his nose, he was capable of striking fear into the hearts of the sturdiest of the men under his command without so much as opening his mouth. And he never underestimated the gravity of the responsibility that was his.

Anyone coming into his office as he studied the weather reports would have gleaned no inkling from his poker face of what was going on in his mind. But as he picked up his telephone to summon the morning conference, a decision had already been made. Present at the conference would be his right-hand man, Air Vice-Marshal Sir Robert Saundby (later Air Marshal, and now deceased) who, as deputy chief of Bomber Command, drew up the detailed flight plans for proposed operations.

Nuremberg had for some weeks been high on the list of the British Cabinet's Combined Strategic Targets Committee, to the extent that a raid on the city had recently been planned and then postponed. This time—failing a significant change in the weather forecasts—it was on.

Chapter Two

Shortly after midday on 30th March 1944 the master tele-printer at High Wycombe sent out the first alert signal to Bomber Groups 1, 3, 4, 5 and 6 and also to Pathfinder Group 8. Group commanders were informed in code that the target for the night was to be Nuremberg, and the accompanying order was terse: "Maximum effort . . . All aircraft to operate . . . Full instructions to follow." This curt message was passed to group operations officers and through them to the stations, who in turn transmitted it to squadron commanders. It was the prelude to intense activity on the stations concerned, where the strictest security measures were immediately put into force. All outgoing telephone calls were blocked and all incoming calls were intercepted, virtually cutting the stations off from the outside world as the preparations began.

The routine was the same thoughout the groups, and everyone had something to do. On the squadrons, bomb trolleys and petrol bowsers crawled out towards the flights in readiness, and the Lancasters and Halifaxes which were to take part in the operation were given half-hour air tests over their aerodromes. Brief as they were, the tests were scrupulously thorough and, as was the rule before any raid, navigational instruments, radar and wireless equipment, guns and bomb doors were checked with the greatest care. Suspected faults were reported to ground-crews and given prompt attention amid the speculation that was not unnaturally rife before a raid. Where was this one to be . . .? Everyone from the top man down to the cookhouse erk knew that it was going to be 'a big one', of course; but it was the ground-crews who hazarded most of the guesses, trying to judge the destination from the bomb-load and the amount of petrol the planes would be carrying. Quite often their surmises were not too wide of the mark. They knew, for instance, that high loads and full tanks usually meant the Ruhr or some such target not too far into Germany; and low loads, to conserve to the limit the bombers' petrol, indicated a deep-penetration flight. It was certain, therefore, that this raid would be of the latter variety.

If the aircrews were curious, they knew that they would be briefed in due course. In the meantime, having completed their air tests, they went to lunch and tried not to dwell too much on the coming operation. Most of them had struck at Berlin only a few nights earlier, when nine per cent of the force had been lost, and they had no illusions about the night's work ahead of them no matter what the target. A beer or two might have helped them through their meal, but the majority preferred to forego their customary beverage. It was not just that there was no place in an operational bomber for a fuddled head; experience had taught them the discomfort of a full bladder on a long trip. No one relished having to make use of the Elsan toilet, back in the fuselage, in cumbersome flying kit and with the aircraft rolling and pitching.

Later, these men would have to go through what they considered the worst part of any raid – the waiting between briefing and take-off time: standing around aimlessly in the smoke-filled atmosphere of a crew-room until the canvas-topped lorries trundled them out to their aircraft. It was always a time of great tension, when the few jokes that were cracked would be too forced and too loud. Stomach muscles would be taut, and the chain-smoked cigarettes would strike dryly at the throat. But that was still some hours away and the crews were not yet keyed up, many of them commenting on the increasing whine of the wind and the heavy rain clouds that hung ominously over their airfields – not seriously believing that the operation would go ahead.

The weather did seem to be worsening, with a threat of snow and sleet that strengthened the feeling that the proposed raid would eventually be scrubbed. A few optimists were of the opinion that it might even be cancelled before their pilots, navigators and bomb-aimers were called to the navigation briefing which always preceded the main crew briefing – a preliminary gathering at which the target was announced in good time for navigators and bomb-aimers to draw up their individual charts.

So the aircrews conjectured idly about the target, but with decreasing expectation that there really would be an operation that night.

There was no such doubt in the big operations room at High Wycombe, where Harris had summoned a conference with his advisory staff. Among those present were the Command's navigation leader, bombing leader, radar leader, signals leader, and flak and intelligence experts. It was at this pre-planning conference that the Commander-in-Chief gave the weight of the force that was to strike Nuremberg, together with a rough estimate of the number of aircraft to be employed.

An outline of the flight plan the bombers were to follow to and from their target was drawn on the huge wall-map of Western Europe – and there was undisguised surprise in the eyes of Sir Robert Saundby as he scrutinised the red tape which, wheeling round the marking pins, traced the bombers' course. From a dead-reckoning position of 51°50N 2°30E – off the Naze – where the force was to rendezvous, the tape streaked in a south-easterly direction to cross the enemy coast near Bruges. With no change of course, it then went on to Charleroi in Belgium; and from there it stretched in an arrow-straight line that represented nearly 250 miles to Fulda, to the north-east of Frankfurt. At Fulda – the final turning point – the force would swing on to a south-easterly heading for the bomb-run on Nuremberg.

Saundby noted with mounting apprehension the inflexible course to which the Lancasters and Halifaxes would be committed once they reached their first turning point at Charleroi . . . a course which he knew would take them dangerously close to the known bases of two German nightfighter beacons.

It was a puzzling flight plan – and even more so when seen in retrospect, particularly in view of what Harris was to say at a later date in his book *Bomber Offensive*. There he recorded that in the month prior to the Nuremberg raid he decided that because of mounting casualties he must, whenever possible, avoid sending single streams of bombers on deeppenetration raids since such streams could be easily plotted by the Germans and intercepted before reaching their target. The alternative, he wrote, was to divide the striking force and either send the two parts to different targets or both to the same target but by different routes, thus confusing the enemy's air defences and making it more difficult for the German controllers to plot the raid. Yet here, for Nuremberg, was a plan to send a large force on a long flight in what was virtually a straight line.

Glancing at the proposed return route the bombers were to follow after the raid, Saundby marked with equal concern that but for two slight changes it was just about as direct as the outward course. He felt very uneasy about it: but the operations room at Bomber Command headquarters was not the place to query a decision made by the Commander-in-Chief.

Saundby did, however, raise his misgivings with Harris after the conference when the two of them were alone, and he was told that the final decision would in any event depend upon the afternoon Met report – which was not quite the reassurance he was seeking. He knew that the deadline for announcing whether an operation was on or off was four o'clock in the afternoon. In the meantime he was obliged, as deputy Commander-in-Chief, to draw up a detailed flight plan for the operation in accordance with Harris's instructions. But before doing so, he contacted Pathfinder Headquarters at Huntingdon on his 'scrambler' telephone and informed the Air Officer Commanding No. 8 (P.F.F.) Group – Air Vice-Marshal D. C. T. Bennett, D.S.O. – of the proposed route.

Bennett, the outstandingly competent and often outspoken Pathfinder chief, was open in his criticism; and he immediately settled down to working out an alternative flight plan in collaboration with his own meteorological experts. The Pathfinder force, masterminded by Bennett and moulded by him into what was then the world's most powerful and accurate target-finding unit, had come into being only after vigorous opposition from Harris. Not that Harris was against main-force bombers being led by specially selected crack crews. What Harris resolutely opposed was the Air Staff's plan to siphon these crews from their squadrons and form them into a single élite corps. He and his group commanders considered that this would be not only unfair to the other groups but also detrimental to the morale of the squadrons; and throughout the spring and summer of 1942 he fought the proposal tooth and nail. But it was a losing battle. The Chief of Air Staff issued a direct order to Harris, and the Pathfinder group was formed. By 1944 it had become a devastating and effective target-finding force.

Bennett, who was a first-class navigator in his own right, planned his route to Nuremberg in the operations room of Pathfinder Headquarters, where there were two great maps. One stretched across an entire wall of the room, and the other – drawn on glass – covered a huge table. The first outline of the routing was plotted on the glass map and the finalised result was then transferred to the wall-map. It was a typical Pathfinder flight plan, replete with 'dog-legs' (zigzagging manoeuvres from the direct line of flight) and other tactical feints aimed at confusing the enemy and making the job of night-fighter interception as difficult as possible; and it was based on the Pathfinder meteorological findings from a report which had been brought back a little earlier by the group's own Mosquito weather-plane.

As was his custom, Bennett formulated the route backwards from the target and was influenced by his preference for down-wind attack – past experience having proved that the tendency in a bombing attack to 'creep back' from the aiming point (or drop bomb-loads short of the target) was even more likely when the bomb-run was made into the wind. And because of the uncertainty of the weather, he decided to lay on three separate types of target marking. They were:

Newhaven: identification of the target by ground-markers dropped visually with the aid of the blind bombing and navigation device known as H2S – a transmitting and receiving set sending out impulses which would bounce back from ground objects and indicate their findings on a screen.

Parramata: markers dropped on H2S alone: to be used only if there was broken cloud obscuring much of the target.

Wanganui: flares floating in the sky: the least accurate of methods but the only possible one if the target was completely covered by cloud.

When he was satisfied that he had left nothing to chance, Bennett sent the proposed Pathfinder route and the suggested methods of marking the target to Bomber Command Headquarters. And there Saundby studied it carefully before submitting it to the main-force commanders – who, by a majority, rejected it.

Among those in opposition was the Honourable Sir Ralph Cochrane, Air Officer Commanding No. 5 Group of Lancasters. Cochrane, perhaps the most brilliant of all the R.A.F.'s wartime air officers and a man with a magnificent brain, was not at all in favour of the 'jinking (zig-zagging) and tactical trickery' on which the Pathfinder route was primarily based. He argued that in practice its only achievement would be to lengthen the flying time to the target and thus greatly increase the risk of night-fighter interception. Furthermore, he and some of his fellow group commanders were certain that a straight route would fool the German controllers into thinking that, as on several previous raids, the bomber stream would suddenly swing off its current course to attack an objective other than the one for which it seemed to be heading.

Bennett, on the other hand, was convinced that a long, straight route would be particularly dangerous because of the weather conditions and the possibility of there being bright moonlight. He argued also that the comparatively little extra time entailed by jinking would not seriously add to the risk of the bombers having to cross the enemy coast in partial daylight on their return trip.

But on this occasion, Bennett was on the losing side. Saundby reported to his chief that the main-force commanders had objected to the Pathfinder route; and Harris, with one of his expressive grunts, agreed that the bombers should fly straight and true to Nuremberg. Nothing in his face gave Saundby the remotest indication of what he was thinking or of what his emotions were concerning the decision he had just made. In fact, though, it had been an agonising one – like all of his decisions that sent his heavies into the hell-skies of Germany. Once a force was airborne there was no question of rescinding the order. One could only hope that the decision had been the right one.

Basically, it was simple. A target had to be bombed, and bombed it would be. This time it was Nuremberg. The only thing that was different was that the plan for saturating Nuremberg with nearly 3000 tons of high explosive and incendiary bombs was abandoning most of the tactics which had for so long governed Bomber Command's operations. For once, there was to be no bluffing. Instead, an almost direct route with virtually no feints – despite the fact that the need for diversionary ploys had been made uncomfortably clear only a month earlier, when an attack on Leipzig had cost seventy-eight bombers ... the Command's highest loss rate to date. If there were any misgivings about the present plan, however, there was still the possibility that the raid would have to be postponed.

But by the four o'clock deadline the afternoon weather reports were to hand, and they showed no appreciable change. Their only additional information was that on take-off visibility would be poor at most bases, but not bad enough to prevent the bombers from getting airborne; and there was a chance that the strong westerly winds calculated to be behind the planes for most of the outward trip would reach speeds of up to ninety miles an hour. The latter point was the most important, for wind speeds were a vital factor in the timing of a raid. If they had ninety-miles-an-hour winds behind them, Lancasters and Halifaxes were capable of hurtling into Germany, throttles wide, at speeds which would astound night-fighters and baffle flak batteries. Could one take a chance on it, though? The Met men thought not. In the final analysis they preferred their original forecast of wind speeds of between forty and fifty miles per hour, and the flight plan was therefore tailored to complement this assumption. It was a significant decision.

Shortly after four o'clock, Saundby was handed the latest Met report and was told by Harris that the raid was on. The bomber chief went on to say that he did not think the weather would be as bad as the Met people thought. He believed it was possible that the wind would drop.

And so Harris committed himself to a calculated gamble that was to prove disastrous.

Chapter Three

After leaving the Commander-in-Chief, Saundby got together with his expert assistants and drew up the final flight plan for the Nuremberg operation. It was substantially the same as that proposed at the morning conference, and it made no provision for any of the large-scale diversions which had been so successful in cutting bomber losses in the past. But in a half-hearted bid to fox the German defences, a small force of Halifaxes was being detailed to lay mines off Texel and in the Heligoland Bight; and fifty-one Mosquitos from No. 8 (P.F.F.) Group were to attack ten other targets, mostly in the Ruhr, some of them with orders to shoot-up night-fighter aerodromes in the area.

Saundby then telephoned Bennett and informed him, to the Pathfinder chief's astonishment, that his routing had been overruled by the man at the top. He went on to explain that some of the main-force commanders had objected to it and that Harris had decided to test their theory that the German night-controllers would be unlikely to believe that the bombers were in fact flying direct to their target. Bennett again protested vigorously but eventually had to submit, although he was far from happy about having to send his Pathfinder force on such a route.

By now the master teleprinter at Bomber Command Headquarters was relaying Harris's orders to the bomber groups, alerting them that the raid was definitely to be carried out. Group commanders were informed that the duration of the attack would be from 0105 hours to 0122 hours, during which time Nuremberg was to be saturated with high explosives and incendiaries. The weather forecast given to them was that of the afternoon report, with its warning to Groups 4 and 6 to expect valley fog on return and its expectation of a heavy, overcast sky over Germany with thick layers of cloud near to the target. They were also told that they could expect large amounts of strata cumulus to 8000 feet, with a risk of patchy medium cloud at 15,000 to 16,000 feet.

On the bomber squadrons mess orderlies were preparing the tables for the evening meal when the loudspeaker systems blared, "Attention. Attention. All pilots, navigators and bomb-aimers to report to main briefing room at fifteen hundred hours . . . Attention . . . All pilots . . ." But the repeat of the summons was drowned in the babble of conversation it had triggered off. Now the spring was coiled. Nerves already raw from the Leipzig and Berlin raids became taut. Some crews cursed, and others greeted the alert with ribaldry; but most merely shrugged resignedly. There was nothing they could do about it. It was what they were here for. Another 'op'; another brush with death.

Most of the wartime bomber stations were designed on the same lines, and what took place at one was duplicated at others. Under the tin roofs of the long, wide Nissen huts that were used as briefing rooms the aircrews assembled. Some of the men sprawled on wooden benches while others, who couldn't find seats or were too edgy to sit still, crowded against the walls. Many of them were in their late teens and a few were in their thirties, but the majority were in their twenties. For several it would be their first raid, and the worry showed on their faces. But the veterans displayed no emotion, though inwardly they felt the familiar nervous tension. They had done it before; they knew what it was all about – and the knowledge chilled them.

In all of these widespread briefing rooms the babble of voices would fade when the Group Captains and their Wing Commanders entered; and the atmosphere would become electric as the target was revealed.

After the moment of revelation, the reaction in one such room was typical of that in others. In the small silence following the announcement a bomb-aimer was heard to whisper complainingly to his navigator, "Blimey. It's a helluva way down, isn't it?" To which the reply was:

"It's a sticky one all right ... Bloody hell!"

But the men who were most disturbed were those who had just returned from leave, having travelled overnight without proper sleep. They viewed the prospect of a long and dangerous mission deep into Germany with a perceptible lack of enthusiasm, knowing only too well that weariness slowed their reactions and made them more vulnerable to the lurking German night-fighters at a time when a heartbeat's hesitation could mean the difference between living and dying. And in this situation was the crew of D-Dog, a Pathfinder Lancaster of No. 156 Squadron, operating from Upwood, near Ramsey. Captained by Squadron Leader Brooks, a former Hurricane pilot, most of the men were on their second tour of operations. They were therefore no newcomers to the game, and they bitterly regretted that they had come back in time to go on this raid without the benefit of a full night's rest.

There was little time to dwell on such matters, however, as the briefing continued with information about the target and details of the proposed attack. Nuremberg, the crews were told, was an important industrial city with a population of 350,000 – a little larger than Edinburgh, a little smaller than Leeds. In this centre of general and electrical engineering was the famous M.A.N. works, which produced land armaments of all kinds – from heavy tanks and armoured cars to Diesel engines; and it was stressed that this factory had become doubly important since many of the Berlin tank works had been destroyed in earlier raids and the huge M.A.N. factory at Augsberg had also been practically wiped out. Additionally, there were two other important factories in Nuremberg – the G. Mueller works, which made special ball-bearings for magnetos, and the Siemens Schuckert-werke, which manufactured electric motors, searchlights, and firing devices for mines. The large Siemens factory in Berlin had been damaged during recent air attacks on the city, crews were reminded, and the firm's plant in Nuremberg had therefore assumed a vital role in the enemy's war effort.

Squadron commanders then took over from intelligence officers to say that the six bomber groups engaged in this operation would rendezvous over the North Sea at a point approximately 51°50N 2°30E and from there fly in a south-easterly direction to 50°30N 4°36E. The force would then turn port and fly east to 50°32N 10°36E, where it would turn on to a south-easterly course for Nuremberg. After the raid, the bombers were to fly due south from Nuremberg to 49°N 11°5E and then to a point 48°30N 9°20E. From there they would fly a course 50°01N 10°E to cross the English coast at 50°40N 0°45W, near Selsey Bill.

The battle order for the attack was as follows:

No. 1 Group: 181 aircraft from Nos. 12, 100, 101, 103, 166, 460, 550, 576, 625 and 626 Squadrons.

No. 3 Group: 59 aircraft from Nos. 15, 75, 90, 115, 149, 199, 514 and 622 Squadrons.

No. 4 Group: 138 aircraft from Nos. 10, 51, 76, 158, 466, 578 and 640 Squadrons.

No. 5 Group: 203 aircraft from Nos. 9, 44, 49, 50, 57, 61, 207, 463, 467, 617, 619 and 630 Squadrons.

No. 6 Group: 120 aircraft from Nos. 408, 420, 424, 425, 426, 427, 429, 432 and 433 Squadrons.

No. 8 Group: 119 aircraft from Nos. 7, 35, 83, 97, 105, 109, 139, (P.F.F.) 156, 405, 582, 627 and 692 Squadrons.

No. 100 Group: 15 Mosquitos to take part in intruder operations in (Special Duties) support of the bomber stream. To seek out night-fighters and destroy them.

Before the main force reached Nuremberg, nine Mosquitos were to make a feint attack on Cologne between 2355 hours and 0007 hours. And a second force of twenty Mosquitos was to drop spoof fighter flares, 'window' (the metallised paper strips which disrupted enemy radar) and target indicators on Kassel between 0026 hours and 0028 hours. This, it was hoped, would fool the German controllers into thinking that the main attack would be somewhere in the Ruhr and so lead them to order the bulk of their fighters to that area.

At 0059 hours two Mosquitos were to mark Nuremberg with green target illuminators, and eight other Mosquitos would bomb the city one minute later. These aircraft were to release four bundles of 'window' per minute. The main force was also to use 'window', dropping it at the rate of one bundle a minute and increasing it to two per minute when the planes were within thirty miles of the target.

As an additional aid to navigation, red route-markers were to be dropped at 50°46N 06°06E (approximately northeast of Aachen) on the outward flight.

Zero hour on Nuremberg for the main force was to be 0110 hours; but five minutes before that, twenty-four Pathfinder Lancasters – their bomb-aimers using the H2S blind-bombing device – were to release marker illuminators on the city. They were to be followed by a sixty-seven-strong wave of supporters, who were to spray the target with more indicators. Then, at 0107 hours, six Pathfinder aircraft were to release yet more markers; and behind them would come twenty-three 'blind' backers-up who would further expose the target with illuminators from 0109 hours to 0122 hours.

The duration of the entire attack was planned to be from 0105 hours to 0122 hours, with the main onslaught occurring between 0110 hours and 0122 hours.

Bomb-aimers were warned that with a forecast wind speed of sixty miles per hour at 21,000 feet over Nuremberg in direction 280° they would have to be snappy with their bombing. And pilots were told that the wind speed was expected to increase to seventy miles per hour over the

French coast on the way home. With visibility likely to deteriorate, it was impressed on them that they would have no time to waste on the return trip.

The success of any big raid depended on its concentration. German anti-aircraft guns used short-wave electricity for their prediction, which meant that if one British plane went over every five minutes each gun would pick up and concentrate on that single aircraft – as would the night-fighters. But if all the aircraft went over more or less simultaneously, neither the guns nor the night-fighters could select a specific target. Concentrated attacks therefore kept losses down – quite apart from the devastation created below when all the aircraft bombed together. But concentrated flying when a large force was involved was a tricky business with hazards of its own. To avoid collisions, each aircraft was given a fixed height at which to fly: but when attacked, it was rarely possible for a plane to stick to its scheduled height and many a bomber would unwittingly corkscrew into another in fleeing from a German night-fighter. It was just one more thing for aircrews to worry about.

And after the briefing the men had little else to do but think of what awaited them. When they had drawn up their individual flight plans, crews discussed the latest intelligence reports on the location and concentration of flak batteries and night-fighter stations along their route and the known terrors they would have to face. They knew, for instance, that because 'window' had so successfully confused radar flak-prediction the Germans had for some time been employing the box-barrage system whereby a particular area through which the British bombers would have to fly was subjected to intense and heavy indiscriminate fire. Because the Germans were taking pot luck, it was pointless for the bombers to attempt evasive action. Indeed, the very act of weaving might bring a plane into the path of one of the thousands of shells that were hosing the box. In such a barrage an aircraft was hazarding accurate predicted guns which, while not seeking a specific target, were sending twelve to sixteen heavy-calibre shells a minute into one small section of the sky – each gun hurling a shell into almost the same spot on its own range every three or four seconds.

Crews had been told that if they ran into box-barrage flak they were to ram on extra throttle, drop the nose of their craft and fly straight through. It was a nerve-racking experience. But demoralising and frightening though it was, the box-barrage was less effective in bringing down bombers than the radar-eyed night-fighters. Veteran crews were aware of this and preferred to risk the barrage rather than the hunting fighters. And tonight, they knew, they would encounter both.

Nevertheless, the tension and excitement was of a somewhat different nature from that which normally preceded a raid on Berlin or the Ruhr. Nuremberg was a comparatively unknown target, and there was nothing to suggest that it might turn out to be an even tougher assignment than anything that had gone before. What comments the crews made were mainly confined to the distance they were to fly without any significant course changes or diversions. It was a thought to nag at the already strained nerves of experienced men, many of whom had been flying operationally almost continuously over a short period of time.

Ernest Rowlinson of Northenden, then a twenty-two-year-old sergeant wireless-operator in Lancaster H-Harry of No. 50 Squadron, based at Skellingthorpe, near Lincoln, recalls, "There was the usual back-chat among the crews, but at the same time there was a feeling of tiredness amongst us. My crew had only been on the squadron for a fortnight, yet this was to be our seventh night on flying duties and our fifth operation – one of which was on Berlin a few nights earlier." He remembers that there was surprise expressed by many in the briefing room when the curtain concealing the route was drawn aside to reveal that they would be flying just south of the Ruhr – a hell-spot long referred to by bomber crews as Flak Valley. But anxieties were allayed to some extent when they were told that thick cloud cover was forecast for most of the way.

C. R. Holley of Southall, then a flight-sergeant rear-gunner in No. 156 Squadron, wrote afterwards, "I'd just had, along with my crew, a very welcome seven-days leave. I'd had to get up at 5.30 in the morning on the 30th March to catch a train from Southall which would get me to King's Cross in time for the early train back to Huntingdon. After meeting our bomb-aimer and radar operator Flying Officer Blackadder – a tall, well-built Birmingham man – and our wireless operator Flight Lieutenant 'Robbie' Bagg, I arrived with them at Upwood just after ten that morning to find, to our intense disgust, that we were down for 'ops' that night. Having just spent a hectic week on leave we were all feeling dead beat and in need of a few days' rest. We cursed the clot who put off-leave crews on the 'blood-list'. We were not altogether happy, either, when we saw we were being routed on a few miles south of the Ruhr."

Former Flight Lieutenant Stephen Burrows, D.F.C., of Evesham, then on his second tour of operations as a flight-engineer in Lancaster Y-Yorker of No. 44 Squadron, station-ed at Dunholme Lodge, remembers, "We were told it was to be a 'maximum effort', deep into enemy territory, and this shook us a bit since the Leipzig raid was still fresh in our minds. Although our crews were all second-tour types, we experienced the usual butterfly feeling in our stomachs. 'Bloody hell!' remarks filled the air as crews entered the briefing room and saw the target map."

The rest of Y-Yorker's complement was fairly typical of an R.A.F. crew. Its pilot, Wing Commander F. W. Thompson, D.F.C., A.F.C., from Blackpool, was twenty-seven years of age. The bomb-aimer, twenty-five-year-old Flying Officer William Clegg, was a bank clerk from Manchester. Wireless operator Pilot Officer Peter Roberts, also from Manchester, was a twenty-three-year-old clerk. The mid-upper-gunner, twenty-three-year-old Flight Sergeant

Middleham, was a factory hand from Leeds. Flight Sergeant A. Stancer, the navigator, was a twenty-two-year-old London office clerk. And the rear-gunner, Flight Sergeant J. Hall, was a mill hand from Yorkshire.

For this crew the mission had an added hazard in that they were detailed to take photographs and assess the bombing of the target after they had made their own bombing-run. It meant that they would have to fly back over Nuremberg while the raid was still on – an easy prey for the ground guns and exposed to the risk of being bombed from above by their own comrades. And the latter possibility was not as far-fetched as it sounded. They had already experienced it on a similar mission, when a cluster of incendiaries had ploughed through the wing of their bomber, and the knowledge haunted them.

Without that particular problem but equally perturbed about the planned route was Flight Sergeant Tom Fogaty, D.F.M., pilot of a Lancaster of No. 115 Squadron, operating from Wicthford, near Ely. He says, "Frankly, we were shaken when we saw that we were going straight to Nuremberg without any of the usual diversions, even though we were assured that there would be ten-tenths cloud cover for most of the way." And Fogaty, who won his D.F.M. for bringing back a crippled Stirling bomber after it had been attacked by a night-fighter while bombing Brunswick earlier in the year, was not a man to be easily shaken.

The important thing, during that fraught and seemingly endless period between briefing and take-off, was to try not to brood on possible disaster in its many permutations. It was essential to keep the mind occupied with anything but thoughts of the coming raid – listening to the mess radio, perhaps; writing letters; playing billiards or table-tennis; reading newspapers; or perversely scanning the long 'Missing' lists in *Flight* and *Aeroplane*, searching for familiar names among aircrew casualties from previous operations. But always constantly glancing at the wall clock – willing away the dragging minutes; wishing to be anywhere but on a bomber squadron and yet at the same time impatient to get the action going.

Soon – too soon? not soon enough? – it would be time for the crews to clamber aboard the trucks that would take them to their flights. Then it would all begin to happen.

Chapter Four

Ordering a fleet of Lancasters and Halifaxes to bomb a target was one thing; but it was quite another thing to ensure that they arrived at the right place at the right time. Seeing that they did so was the duty of the Pathfinder force.

Under Bennett's brilliant direction, it was general Pathfinder policy to use H2S for homing in on all targets which were outside the range of another tried and true navigational device known as Oboe. But it was necessary to revert to Oboe for targets in the Ruhr, which was too congested an area for H2S cover.

Oboe – so accurate that it could be used for blind bombing – was, in essence, a scheme for guiding aircraft from the ground. It required two stations, the first of which directed a radio pulse over the centre of the target. Along this the aircraft would travel, the pilot recognising that he was on course by means of a continuous tone-signal transmitted to him from the station. Similarly, signals received as dots on one side of the true course and dashes on the other side would indicate to the station whether or not the aircraft was keeping to the constant radius required to bring it on to the target.

The pulse from the first station was radiated back from the aircraft to the second ground station, which could then make periodic calculations of the plane's progress along the given track by noting the time taken to receive the pulse. Then, as the aircraft approached the point at which it was scheduled to release its bombs, the second station would send out a long dash signal, at the end of which the bomb-aimer would immediately let his cargo drop.

Oboe could guarantee that the bombs would fall within a few hundred yards of the aiming point even on the darkest night through dense cloud. But it had its weaknesses. Like the navigational device called Gee, its dependence on ground stations limited its range to about three hundred and fifty miles. It also had the disadvantage of being able to handle only a single aircraft during the final ten minutes of approach to the target; and another serious drawback was that for those last vital minutes it required the aircraft to fly dead level in order to send out signals, thus making the plane highly vulnerable to enemy guns and fighters.

For these reasons, it was decreed that Oboe should not be used as a blind-bombing device for the entire force committed to the Nuremberg raid but only as a target-finding and marking aid for the lead crews.

Chosen to lead the Pathfinder force were two of the Command's most experienced bomber pilots – Wing Commander Sidney Patrick Daniels, D.S.O., D.F.C. and Bar, Commanding Officer of No. 35 Pathfinder Squadron at Graveley, Huntingdonshire, and his flight commander Squadron Leader Keith Creswell, D.S.O., D.F.C. (both of whom were later awarded Bars to their D.S.O.S). They were to be the primary visual markers, responsible for finding the target and marking it for their supporters in the Pathfinder detail. Their Lancasters would be well stocked with flares, and when these had been released over the aiming point the illuminator-planes would sweep in to drop their sticks of flares across it. On their tails would come the primary markers – accurate bomb-aimers – who would drop target-indicators on the aiming point, which would by now be visually identifiable in the brilliance of the flares. Following them, the backers-up would release more target-indicators on the glittering 'Christmas-tree' below, so that the main-force bombers would have a mark to aim at throughout the raid.

Daniels, as commanding officer of the squadron, was not obliged to take an active part in the operation; but he had decided to elect himself after seeing the route the force was to take. Although he was only twenty-three years old at the time, no one knew better than he the burden of responsibility that rested on the leaders of the crack crews of Bomber Command at the best of times. In a situation as seemingly foolhardy as this, he certainly had no intention of opting out – which was very much in character for a man who had proved himself an outstandingly brave officer and an exceptionally skilled bomber pilot in over eighty operations, mainly against some of the most heavily defended targets in Germany.

He had felt qualms about the route to Nuremberg as soon as he had begun to study it on the wall-map of his squadron's briefing room, noting with amazement that it either ran through or was incredibly close to almost every known German night-fighter assembly beacon south of the Ruhr. It just did not seem possible to him or his flight commander that such a route could have been devised by Pathfinder Headquarters. But apparently it had, and he wanted to know why.

On leaving the briefing room he had driven straight to his office in the station's administration block and contacted Pathfinder Command on the 'scrambler' telephone, protesting to Bennett about the course his men were being ordered to fly. He complained strongly over the absence of spoof targets and warned that if the force was compelled to fly the planned route it might well suffer "the highest chop rate ever".

But Bennett, who couldn't have been more in sympathy with the squadron commander, had been able to do no more than explain how the proposed Pathfinder route had been rejected by Bomber Command.

Shortly after six o'clock that evening – three hours before No. 35 Squadron was due to taxi on to the runway at Graveley – Daniels, having voiced his objections and accepted the inevitable, briefed the men he was going to lead. He opened with a general pep-talk in which he emphasised the importance of the target they were going to attack, and then he gave details of the types of flares and illuminators the Lancasters would carry and the precise times at which they would mark Nuremberg. With a billiards cue in his hand he went over the route, tapping the wall-map to indicate places along the course which were dangerously close to heavily defended areas, and he ended with a brief warning on the observance of specified flight heights.

"Eight hundred aircraft are going to Nuremberg tonight," he said, "and if we are to avoid collisions it's important that you keep to your heights. Be particularly alert, and weave your aircraft into gentle banks so that the gunners can get a better chance of seeing any night-fighters that may be around. Good luck, and a good trip."

Chapter Five

German night-fighter airfields stretched in a great lethal arc from northern France, through Belgium and Holland, tailing eastwards across northern and western Germany, to Berlin; and they were commanded by one of Hitler's most capable officers, General 'Beppo' Josef Schmid. To General Schmid, who was also chief of the supreme command position – the 1st Fighter Corps – with headquarters at Treuenbrietzen, south of Berlin, had fallen the unenviable and apparently hopeless task of defending Germany against night-and-day air attacks.

The British air assault on Berlin itself had been launched in the middle of November 1943, when on the night of the 18th/19th over four hundred bombers dropped 1500 tons of bombs on the city with a loss of only nine of the force. On that same night a force of 325 aircraft dropped 852 tons of bombs on Mannheim. It was the first time that two heavy raids were carried out in one night.

The bombing of Berlin continued until the night of 24th/25th March 1944, by which time sixteen attacks – some very heavy – had been accomplished. In twelve out of fifteen major raids the total casualties recorded in German documents were 5166 killed and 18,432 injured. The number of missing was unknown. Damage reported in seven of these raids gave an aggregate of 15,635 houses destroyed or severely damaged; and by March 1944 about one and a half million Berliners were homeless.

In the four major attacks on Berlin carried out in November 1943 the 'missing' rate for British bombers reached only the surprisingly low proportion of four per cent; and in all the major attacks on German targets, including Berlin, it was no more than 3·6 per cent. But in the following month, despite bad weather, the German night-fighter force clearly increased its efficiency. For in most of the big attacks, which included four more on Berlin, it succeeded in intercepting the main bomber force while it was still on the way to its objective. As a consequence, British losses were appreciably higher and the 'missing' rate in the Berlin attacks rose to 4·8 per cent. The scales had tipped decisively in favour of the German night-fighters, supported by anti-aircraft fire that had become more effective than usual.

But although German flak was now taking its toll, there was no doubt in anyone's mind that the night-fighters were the main cause of the high losses being suffered by Harris's bomber fleets. Indeed, the Deputy Director of Science at the Air Ministry was moved to observe that when routes over northern Germany were followed the difficulty of evading the fighters was now evident.

The reference to northern Germany was not without significance. In the ill-fated Leipzig attack, night-fighters had accounted for nearly all of the seventy-eight missing British aircraft: but the extent to which they were committed to the defence of northern Germany was evidenced by the relative lack of activity on the southern route followed by part of the surviving force on its homeward journey. And it was this that led Bomber Command to change not only its tactics but also its strategy. Attacks on Berlin would be virtually discontinued. Instead, the emphasis would be on raiding towns in the southern part of Germany – with Nuremberg as the chief target.

It was against this background that General Schmid had to plan and execute his interceptions. Almost nightly he was compelled to throw an air umbrella of night-fighters above the cities and towns of Germany to cushion them against the bombs which rained down more heavily with each raid: and he had no illusions about the formidable task that had been entrusted to him. He also knew precisely what the enemy was trying to achieve.

His chief adversary in England, Sir Arthur Harris, had convinced the Allied Combined Operational Planning Committee that the best way to paralyse the German industrial effort was to destroy the houses of German workers. In January 1944, Harris had reinforced his argument (as recorded in the third and last volume of the officially commissioned history of the Royal Air Force in the Second World War) by declaring that of the twenty towns in Germany associated mainly with the aircraft industry ten had been attacked by his Command, which had destroyed over a quarter of their built-up areas. These assaults, he had asserted, had cost the enemy one million man years or thirty-six per cent of the potential industrial effort in twenty-nine towns.

Whatever else Harris's Command had done, it had certainly made a mockery of Goering's boast that no bombs would ever fall on the Third Reich: and that was the cross General Schmid had to bear as the long arm of Bomber Command reached further into Germany.

To combat these night raids, Schmid had under his direct command four main night-fighter divisions: No. 1 Jagddivision at Berlin-Döberitz, commanded by Oberst Hajo Herrman; No. 2 Jagddivision at Stade, commanded by General-Major Max Ibel; No. 3 Jagddivision at Deelen, commanded by General-Major Walter Grabmann; and No. 7 Jagddivision at Schleissheim, near Munich, commanded by General-Major Huth. These divisions were subdivided into Groups, each with forty to sixty aircraft. Three or four Groups formed a night-fighter Geschwader (squadron) – the highest combat unit. And Groups were in turn split into Staffels (echelons) of eight to ten night-fighters—roughly half the strength of an R.A.F. operational bomber squadron – each Staffel commanded by a Staffelkapitan of the rank of Leutnant, Oberleutnant or Hauptmann.

Geschwaders were referred to in the abbreviated form of

N.J.G. (Nachtjagdgeschwader), preceded by Roman numerals to denote the number of the Group and followed by Arabic numerals to identify the Staffel.

To engage the bombers while his night eagles climbed to intercept them General Schmid had an elaborate and effective network of heavy and light flak zones interspaced with powerful searchlight lanes. Strategically situated among them were the main radio beacons that directed his fighters into the bomber stream, each tower close to a main light-flashing beacon over which the airborne twin-engined Me.110s and Ju.88s orbited. The tactic was for them to circle the beacon while waiting to be brought under control from the ground, when they would be guided on a reciprocal course to the leading enemy bombers.

First indications of air activity would come from the radar operators – those on the huge Freya sets being depended upon for early warning, and those on the Würzburg sets readying themselves to direct the night-fighters. The Freya system had twice the range of the Würzburg, but the Würzburg had a thinner and more accurate beam.

Usually the night-fighters worked in pairs, Fighter No. 1 being directed by the Würzburg operators while Fighter No. 2 continued to circle the radio beacon at the reported height of the incoming bombers. When contact had been established by Fighter No. 1 he would be released from ground control, which would then take over Fighter No. 2. Radio silence would be maintained except when it was necessary for a pilot to answer specific questions from the ground controller.

The methods of the night-fighters were simple and effective. They would carry out their search as directed from the ground, flying slightly lower than the estimated altitude of the bomber so that they could look upwards for the dark silhouette of their prey against the starlight. On visually identifying a bomber they would fly below it, either to port or starboard, and fire into its wings to set the petrol tanks ablaze. They would then dive sharply away to avoid the tremendous concussion of the exploding bomb-load. Their range on a dark night would be from about one hundred to one hundred and fifty yards, but it could sometimes be as short as thirty-five yards. On a bright night it might be more than two hundred yards.

Whether the night of 30th/31st March 1944 would be bright or dark it was too soon to tell as preparations began on General Schmid's flak and searchlight sites for another possible battle with the British Lancasters and Halifaxes. Fresh stocks of heavy calibre shells for the big 8.8cm anti-aircraft guns were neatly stacked in the gun-pits in readiness; and searchlight-unit electricians made their final check on the massive power plants to ensure that when the switches were thrown there would be dazzling arms of light to grope among the clouds for intruders. Steel-helmeted spotters adjusted the night lenses of their range-finders and settled down to scan the evening sky, noting that the dark and heavy rain-clouds that had been hovering all day were now slowly clearing.

For most of the day an all-weather front had lain across the greater part of the Reich; but now, as the clouds rolled back, there was some promise that the crescent moon that had been lurking behind them might eventually break through. It was enough to encourage the men responsible for combating enemy raiders to believe that it could turn out to be a mercifully quiet night after all. They knew from experience that the British preferred pitch-black nights with thick protecting cloud for the launching of their 'terror raids': so if the weather improved and the moon appeared, it was probable that no bombers would come and that the men would be 'stood-down' to the warmth of their quarters.

This was the hope of twenty-three-year-old Leutnant Wilhelm Seuss, pilot of an Me.110 of the 17th Squadron of the 5th Night-Fighter Wing, based at Erfurt, near Weimar, in Saxony. Leutnant Seuss, his wireless-operator Corporal Bruno Zakrsewski and his air-gunner Senior Lance-

Corporal Fritz Sagner all had a special reason for wanting the night to be undisturbed – for in a few hours they were due to go on leave after a long, relentless spell of night-fighting. Seuss recalls that he glanced at his watch and strolled to the door of his hut to anxiously study the sky. What he saw reassured him, and he did not seriously think that there was much chance of the leave being cancelled. Within the next few hours, he reckoned, the moon would appear: and it had been his experience since the autumn of 1943 that British long-range attacks took place only under adverse weather conditions for the defenders – when there was thick cloud over night-fighter bases, full cloud over the target, and no moonlight. It didn't look as though it was going to be that sort of night.

Similar thoughts occupied Hauptmann Fritz Lau, thirty-three years of age and flight-commander of No. 4 Flight, No. 1 Night-Fighter Squadron, which had just arrived at Loan-Athies. His group had been transferred from St. Diezier, in France, after American bombers had attacked the airfield and damaged seven of their aircraft. Lau recalls, "We had the impression that during this particular night we were not likely to go into action because the weather was very clear and a small sickle moon had appeared. Our judgment was that it would be too light for the enemy to try anything."

Soon he and the countless other watchers would know for certain. Meanwhile, in the battle 'opera-houses', as the night-fliers nicknamed their divisional ground-control rooms, women auxiliaries of the Signals Corps adjusted their headphones and laryngophones before placing trays containing thick black crayons within easy reach of the great glass maps in front of them. When the time came, their lithe fingers would fashion bold arrows on the glass as they traced the positions of advancing bombers. But now only their fleeting shadows could be seen from the control rooms as they moved silently behind the massive trans-parent map.

These women were highly trained, and they made up about seventy-five per cent of the personnel of the aircraft-reporting service in the ground-defence organisation of the Luftwaffe. Their plotting was done from curt, precise orders which came through their headphones from skilled fighter-control and radar officers who had been chosen for their ability to visualise the nightly air battles being waged above them.

Seriously hampered more often than not by the radio-jamming devices operated by British aircrews and by the decoy moves of bomber streams, the officers had to quickly and accurately assess the probable objective of a force. Only then could the fighter squadrons be brought swiftly together in the correct air-box and at the right time to intercept the bombers. Vital to this task was the accurate filtering of their observations – a skill partly intuitive but developed out of long experience.

At control headquarters the continuous flow of information from the various divisional command areas had to be quickly sifted and appraised to distinguish between the genuine, the doubtful and the completely false. Dummy courses flown by the bombers had to be speedily recognised; nuisance raids had to be identified; and the stepped-up height levels of the bombers had to be calculated. A wrong order or a faulty assumption would give the invaders precious minutes in which to swing on to their actual turning point before those in the control rooms realised their mistake.

An air plot would gradually be compiled from dead-reckoning calculations by former officers of the German Merchant Navy – each of whom was the holder of a Captain's certificate. They would work out the possible attack targets from the moment of a bomber fleet's detection, always allowing for variations and diversions in the courses.

Strikingly printed in red on the plotters' maps were the locations of radio beacons over which night-fighters would assemble once the direction of an enemy force had been fixed within reasonable doubt. Two of these – Ida, situated a few miles south-east of Aachen, and Otto, a few miles west of Frankfurt – were in the direct path of Harris's Nuremberg force.

General Schmid could not yet know that, but he was prepared for some such eventuality. He had made a careful analysis and reconstruction of the tactics employed by the British bomber chief, and he had noted that since Leipzig there had seemed to be a marked reluctance on the part of the enemy Air Marshal to continue his raids on Berlin and other cities in the north. From this, he had rightly assumed that from now on the bombers would try the southern route: and he was ready for them with a faster version of the Ju.88 – the Mark R2 – equipped with a vastly more efficient type of radar.

Above all, this latest radar – the Lichtenstein SN2 – could penetrate the 'window' screens dropped by the bombers . . . the only radar able to do so since 'window' had been used with such devastating effect during the Battle of Hamburg in July 1943. At that time, because of the confusion 'window' had caused, the German radar-controlled searchlights had weaved aimlessly in all directions and the fire from the ground guns – though heavy – had been badly aimed. As a result, only twelve British bombers out of a force of seven hundred and ninety-one had been brought down.

It would be different now. For apart from the SN2, the v.h.f. radio-direction stations which fed information to Schmid's night-fighters had been tremendously boosted, and there was no doubt that reportage on the movements of bombers would come through loud and clear despite British jamming devices.

There was the human element too. Schmid was particularly fortunate in having among his night-fighter divisional commanders an outstandingly skilful and experienced man, Oberst im Generalstab Johannes Janke. Chief of Staff of No. 7 Jagddivision, with headquarters at Schleissheim, Janke was responsible for the night and day air defence of southern Germany; and he had gathered around him a brilliant team of electronics experts whose direction-finding techniques had put the 7th Jagddivision ahead of all the others. That night he was ready for anything that might come into his territory. The crescent moon, which would be his ally in the event of a British raid, was growing bigger and brighter; and in his battle control rooms there was an atmosphere of calm efficiency. Every officer and every operator knew exactly what he had to do: but there was no indication as yet that anyone would be called upon to do anything.

The tension and excitement that would electrify the control rooms when the great guessing game began were still some time away. In the meantime, Janke and his No. 7 Jagddivision waited.

Chapter Six

On the rain-swept bomber airfields in England Lancasters and Halifaxes taxied out from their dispersal bays, lumbering one after another in a long, snaky line. Flashes of red-yellow flame belched from their exhausts and stained the darkness as engines were run up and eased back. Luminous clocks set in instrument panels showed that it was ten o'clock – 2200 hours. These planes would be taking off a little after the hour; but from other fields the take-off had been just before the hour. It depended upon how far each squadron had to fly to the rendezvous with the main force.

The steadily falling rain on the majority of airfields had thinned the numbers of ground-crews and Waafs who normally gathered at the top of the runways to give operational aircrews a farewell wave; but no airfield was without at least a few watchers who had braved the elements.

Each main-force Lancaster was carrying a full bomb-load consisting of one 4000lb high-explosive 'cookie' and between 5000lb and 6000lb of incendiaries. The incendiaries, made up of 32lb oil-bombs and caskets of stick clusters, were stowed in the wing racks.

The Halifaxes of No. 4 Group, which had to accommodate extra fuel to feed their radial engines, carried a correspondingly lighter but no less lethal load of four 1000lb high-explosive bombs and between 2000lb and 3000lb of incendiaries.

Parked some distance from airfield runways were mobile

control wagons. When their Aldis signal lamps flickered green, aircraft throttle levers were rammed open, engines thundered at full pitch, and the bombers rolled smoothly down the mile-long flare-paths, gathering speed with each second. Pregnant with their deadly cargo, they seemed to lift reluctantly and then climb laboriously into the night, their navigational lights twinkling like fireflies.

The watchers below felt the earth tremble in the crescendo of ear-shattering waves of sound released by the aircraft in their take-off, and soon they could glimpse only sinister shadowy shapes that quickly dwindled as the squadrons climbed ever higher, their engines beating out a throbbing, monotonous concerto.

In the flimsy security of their blacked-out compartments in the noses of the aircraft, navigators and bomb-aimers settled down over their plotting charts; and in the terrifying isolation of the rear-turrets, gunners thumbed the red switches on the trigger controls of their four Browning .303s to the 'Fire' position. Firmly, through the thickness of gloves, their fingers felt for the knobs that controlled the brilliance of their graticle sights and carefully adjusted them. Too much glare and their night vision would be seriously affected in the few seconds they would have to focus on a German fighter – provided that they saw it before it saw them. And already the cold seeped through their electrically-heated flying suits in short, sharp needle-thrusts.

Far below and behind them, the English coastline blurred into a drifting charcoal haze as the aircraft climbed to their own operating height. Bombing altitudes for all groups had been prearranged to minimise the risk of collisions, the minimum and maximum heights for each being:

No. 1 Group – 19,000 feet to 23,000 feet; No. 3 Group – 17,000 feet to 25,000 feet; No. 4 Group – 19,000 feet to 20,000 feet; No. 5 Group – 19,000 feet to 22,000 feet; No. 6 Group – 18,000 feet to 23,000 feet; and No. 8 Group – 15,000 feet to 20,000 feet.

Red route-markers set to flare at 12,000 feet were to be dropped on the outward journey at 50°46N 06°06E.

In the port inner engine of many of the bombers had been fitted a powerful microphone which was connected to the wireless-operator's transmitter set. At briefing, the wireless-operators of these aircraft had each been given a specific waveband on which to concentrate. If they happened on anything that sounded like instructions to German night-fighters, they were to tune in their transmitters and clamp down on the morse key – thus sending blasts of engine-noise into the wavelength being used by the German ground controllers.

Several of the bombers had been installed with Fishpond – a radar set operated by the wireless-operator and capable of locating aircraft within a five-mile radius, showing them as blips on the screen. It naturally picked up the rest of the force, but any blip that did not conform to the pattern of the bomber stream could, with some degree of confidence, be considered to represent a hostile plane.

But there were to be other problems before Fishpond came into its own. As the squadrons climbed to make the rendezvous over the North Sea at approximately 51°50N 2°30E – some miles off Frinton-on-Sea – navigators in the leading bombers began to get a hint of the terrifically high wind-speeds that would be additional to the other perils awaiting them. Some registered as much as eighteen degrees of drift and had to alter course accordingly after checking and counter-checking with Gee – a radar navigation device whereby ground stations in England transmitted a signal to receiving sets in aircraft – that their calculations were right. And as they climbed higher through swirling mists of cumulo-nimbus cloud the wind seemed to whip itself into a frenzy, buffeting and jolting them like corks in a mountain torrent.

On reaching the assembly point, all navigation lights were switched off and the force wheeled on course for the enemy coast. Bomb-aimers now began to check their pre-flight settings on the bombing computer boxes and fed into them a new estimated wind-speed and direction, while gunners cocked their Brownings, swallowed the 'pep' pills they had been given earlier to help ward off drowsiness on the long flight into Germany, and commenced keeping vigil from their turrets.

Navigators of aircraft equipped with radar, having taken Gee fixings and made dead-reckoning calculations, noted with increasing anxiety that the wind-speed was now nearly half that of their air-speed – and they knew that the forecasters had slipped up somewhere along the line. Those without radar – and, ironically, they were the least experienced and therefore the ones who needed it most – did not realise what was happening and began unwittingly to fly outside the ordained concentration. Others, unsure of their wind-speed reckonings, checked again and still doubted.

Gradually, the flight plan became chaotic. What should have been a tight 'flying box' two miles wide stretched into an ever-thinning and extremely vulnerable formation of stragglers fifty miles across – an air-box which, by its very width, deprived itself of the protection of a thick curtain of 'window' so essential in confusing the German ground controllers.

But the force flew on, its broken concentration becoming more evident with each air mile. The less-confident navigators now had their aircraft out in front, hurtling further and further away from the safety of the main stream; and behind them flew the doubters, perplexed and baffled by the air plots that were taking shape on their Mercator charts. In the rear came the bulk of Harris's 'heavies', dog-legging desperately to avoid arriving at the first turning point at Charleroi ahead of their E.T.A. (estimated time of arrival).

Yet despite this confusion as the force nosed nearer to the enemy coast, there was still no way of knowing that it was heading for the greatest single air battle the world has ever known. Things were not going according to plan, it was true: but the bomber fleet was committed to an operation and nothing could alter that. Most crews knew by now that the meteorological forecast given to them at the briefing was utterly wrong and entirely misleading. There would be no heavy cloud cover. They would be naked in the moonlight – clearly visible to the German night-fighters. But they had to go on.

In the hooded glow of his engineer's compartment, Flight Lieutenant Steve Burrows checked the ghostly, glowing dials on his panel, although the monotonous beat of Y-Yorker's four engines were an assurance that they were behaving as they should. He moved into the astro-dome and peered out into the darkness, surprised to see that the great pyramids of cloud through which they had been flying were fast disappearing. Ahead were broken, patchy formations – and visibility was rapidly improving.

He stepped down from the transparent blister and glanced over his pilot's shoulder at the altimeter, noting that the needle was creeping over the 17,000-feet notch. Wing Commander F. W. Thompson, who was at the controls of this £75,000-worth of Lancaster aircraft, looked up at the engineer and raised his thumb questioningly. Burrows acknowledged with a reassuring nod of his head, indicating that the engines were performing perfectly.

In the nose of Y-Yorker, Flight Sergeant Stancer frowned over his chart, put down his dividers and leaned across his plotting-desk. From the Gee set in front of him he took another reading and swiftly plotted it, his eyebrows puckering. Then he flicked the switch on his oxygen-mask that activated his intercom system.

"Navigator to skipper," he said. "The Met forecast winds are all bull. Heavy tail winds have given us an incredible ground-speed. Unless we're to be well ahead of our E.T.A. on the next turning point, we'll have to dog-leg. First dog-leg course coming up."

Thompson's response was to ask his navigator if he was quite certain of his calculations.

"Absolutely," Stancer told him.

Thompson then asked whether the Gee set could be malfunctioning, but Stancer assured him that he had checked and re-checked the set and that it was working perfectly.

This piece of information left the Wing Commander with little choice, although he was not at all keen to dog-leg. Y-Yorker would have to alter course 60° port for one minute and then swing 120° back, flying two sides of an equilateral triangle. It would lengthen their time to the first turning point, giving them two minutes to fly to a point they would otherwise have reached in half the time: but other aircraft would be doing the same thing and the collision risk would be high.

Thompson set the new course on his compass and swung the Lancaster in a gentle bank on to the first dog-leg. No sooner had he done so than the intercom crackled again. This time it was the rear-gunner, Flight Sergeant Hall, who reported, "Unidentified aircraft coming towards us port quarter."

Thompson's hands tightened on the control column, ready to throw the Lancaster into a violent corkscrew, when he saw the massive shape of a Halifax as it zoomed over them with a mere twenty-five-yards' clearance.

"Jeeze, that was close!" someone gasped over the inter-com; and then Stancer's matter-of-fact voice came through again to give the last dog-leg, which would take them just over the enemy coast. He would then give a new course for Charleroi.

Harris's heavies were now strewn out in a wide, vulnerable stream between the mouth of the Scheldt and Ostend, and the leading crews cursed the failings of the weather-men as they looked out on a night which was becoming brighter with each air mile they travelled. The heavy cloud cover they had been promised was behind them. Ahead, the stars shone with abnormal clarity from an endless conveyor-belt of black velvet. But worst of all, pilots who took the time to glance upwards could see with horror the vapour trails of other bombers. Some of them had little difficulty in reading the squadron identification letters of aircraft uncomfortably close to them. It brought home to them the chilling fact that if these conditions persisted they would have to shoot their way through to Nuremberg: and not even the foolhardiest of them reckoned much for their chances in a duel with a night-fighter. A fighter, with its heavier calibre machine-guns and cannon, could stay well out of range of their puny .303s and pump shells at them at will.

Such were the thoughts of Sergeant Reginald Cripps, now of Swansea, who was the rear-gunner of L-Love – a Halifax of No. 158 Squadron, based at Lissett, East Yorkshire. L-Love's pilot was Flight Sergeant Stan Windmill, then aged twenty-six, six feet tall and an ex-policeman from London. The bomb-aimer was thirty-five-year-old James Cooper from Glasgow; the wireless-operator twenty-eight-year-old Richard Avery from Bristol; and the flight engineer twenty-three-year-old Peter McKenzie from Islay in the Western Isles. Manning the mid-upper turret was another Glasgow man, thirty-five-year-old Sergeant Matt Wyllie, who was a good fifteen years older than the average bomber gunner.

Cripps, who was later to receive a commission and a D.F.C. on completion of his operational tour, remembers that twenty aircraft from Lissett were detailed for the raid, of which only sixteen became airborne. Four of these turned back because of mechanical failure, four were listed as missing, and only eight completed the mission.

Talking of the approach to the enemy coast, Cripps says, "Visibility was very good and the moon was coming out, so we could easily see the numbers on the aircraft flying near us. To the north and south of the bomber stream there was much searchlight activity as we crossed the coast."

Flying in the stream close to Cripps was the veteran Lancaster G-George of No. 460 Squadron, Royal Australian Air Force. G-George was making its eighty-seventh mission over Germany, and if it survived to do three more operations it would then be flown to Canberra to be exhibited in the Australian National War Museum. On this night it was skippered by Pilot Officer Neal of Melbourne. He and his crew were on their eighth operation, and they were in the battle-proud G-George – with its long history of being a lucky aircraft – because their own plane, K-King, was undergoing a major overhaul.

Although G-George belonged to the R.A.A.F., its crew – apart from Neal and his navigator, Pilot Officer Gourley of Tasmania – was made up of Englishmen. One of them – flight-engineer Sergeant R. E. Holder – recalls, "As we crossed the coast at a height of eighteen thousand feet, climbing towards our operating band of twenty-two thousand feet, we saw a vast change in the weather. The sky in front of us was clear, with hardly a trace of cloud. We expected the usual anti-aircraft fire from the coastal batteries, but there was none. And we spotted many other bombers cruising alongside of us, though normally we never saw them until we neared the target."

Ahead of the bombers, Mosquitos of the Night Striking Force opened the night's proceedings with low-level attacks on the known night-fighter aerodromes at Leiuwarden, Twente, Deelen and Venlo in a bid to keep the fighters grounded. Peeling off from 10,000 feet, the incredibly fast twin-engined Mosquitos weaved through the searchlights and under the technicolored arcs of light flak that was being thrown up at them to rake the night-fighter fields with long bursts of cannon and machine-gun fire. Banking in tight blood-draining turns that made their structure tremble, they flattened out and made repeated runs over the airfields, each time spraying them with tracer and cannon shells.

Almost simultaneously, the force of fifty Halifaxes .detailed to confuse German ground controllers started dropping their mines off Texel and in the Heligoland Bight.

Operation Nuremberg had begun.

Chapter Seven

The powerful ever-alert Würzburg sets, their radar ears cocked fanwise towards the English coast, were the first to detect intense enemy air activity in the Norwich area. Blips flickered in their hundreds on the cathode screens as the British bombers rose from their bases and moved in swarms along an easterly heading. And the German plotters watched them converge over the northern part of the Channel to take a south-easterly course.

At the same time, blips from a smaller British formation appeared in the southern sector of the North Sea.

The supreme command position – the 1st Fighter Corps at Treuenbrietzen – was immediately alerted, and the code-word Fasan (pheasant) was flashed to all German night-fighter squadrons to warn them that raids were imminent. It was the signal for Ju.88s, Messerschmitts and FW.190s on operational stations to be hurriedly loaded with fuel and ammunition for take-off at a moment's notice; and ground-crews on auxiliary airfields rolled out petrol bowsers and ammunition trucks in readiness to refuel and reload fighters that might be forced to land away from their home bases.

The radar screens tracked the first wave of British bombers as it thrust over the Scheldt estuary to the Liège-Florennes line, and at supreme headquarters General Schmid correlated the latest radar reports and decided, correctly, that the smaller stream approaching the Heligoland Bight must consist of mine-laying aircraft. But the feint was too crude to hoodwink him into believing that the main attack would come in the east.

A teleprinter, stuttering suddenly into life, disturbed his train of thought as it tapped out the message "Mosquito aircraft attacking night-fighter aerodromes in Holland". Schmid stroked his chin reflectively and glanced at the wall-clock: half past ten . . . 2230 hours. Everything seemed to point to the British attacking a target in the south or south-east, but it was still possible for them to swing off to the east.

Abruptly, he called for the very latest Met reports. They forecast a clear, starlit night with a crescent moon. Ideal, he thought, for hunting the 'fat dogs'. And the forecast promised that soon – very soon now – the moon would become even brighter.

He hesitated no longer. His fighters would meet the British bombers as they came in. The sky was clear of cloud from the coast inwards, and his pilots – once they were vectored into the bomber stream – would have excellent opportunities for 'cat's-eye' interceptions. There was now no doubt in his mind about the massive air activity detected earlier off the Wash. The British Air Chief Marshal was obviously launching one of his 'maximum effort' raids against the Third Reich.

Without further ado, Schmid gave the order for his Gruppen and Staffels of night-fighters to take off; and then he watched keenly the red blobs of light that lanced across the glass map at the far end of his control room. As radar echoes flicked out in a steady and constant stream from the advancing air-armada and confirmed to the fighter controllers that a mammoth raid was being mounted, he saw the red flashes spreading down the map and noted that Harris's heavies had now passed over the regions of Antwerp and Brussels to the position Luttich, Florennes, where they were making a sudden swing on to an easterly course. Again he looked at the clock: twelve minutes past eleven . . . 2312 hours.

With the red pinpoints of light inexorably advancing, tension in the control room increased. At this stage no one could foresee the ultimate objective of the bombers or what diversions, dummies, or double turns they might yet employ. But it seemed clear that the success or failure of tonight's battle with Bomber Command would depend entirely upon how accurately the fighters could be sluiced into the bomber stream.

General Schmid was aware of the anxious, strained look on the faces of his ground-control officers as they quietly and methodically went about their plotting. On them the fighter pilots would be relying for the latest course changes of the bombers, for their altitude, and for the size, depth and length of the enemy force. And he knew – better, perhaps, than any of them – the chance he had just taken in ordering the night-fighter squadrons airborne: for precious fuel and vital minutes were being lost while they circled their assembly beacons awaiting instructions.

And now reports were coming in that the R.A.F.'s Night Striking Force Mosquitos were making low-level attacks over a wide area: Bonn, Köln-Marburg, Kassel-Plauen, Zwickau, Nordhausen and Frankfurt-am-Main. Others, flying higher, were approaching Mannheim.

Uncertainty began to nag at General Schmid. The real target of the bombers could well be somewhere in the area now under Mosquito attack. On the other hand, these operations might be a carefully planned decoy to lure the bulk of his fighters to that region.

Another message was handed to him: "Spearhead of main enemy formation has changed course at Charleroi and is now flying on a south-easterly heading, height 5000 to 7000 metres." The battle situation was still too fluid, still too confused, for him to commit himself to a definite forecast of the enemy's objective, but some of his earlier doubts were now eased. If the bombers continued a little longer on their present course they would cross the Rhine directly over radio-beacon Ida, where the vanguard of his fighters was now orbiting. To the south of Ida was radio-beacon Otto, where more fighters were circling.

He strode across to the map, convinced again that the attack would come in the south. But he was nevertheless deeply puzzled. It seemed to him incredible that the British had chosen a night with brilliant moonlight for the launching of such a large-scale raid. All of the latest meteorological reports supported this view, and he could only conclude that whoever had planned the attack had been ill-served with weather forecasts. The British must surely have been expecting cloud cover and little or no moonlight. Well, they would be disappointed. They were going to meet the biggest night-fighter defence effort ever made by the Luftwaffe.

Tonight, Schmid assured himself, would be the Night of the Big Kill.

At Schleissheim, Oberst im Generalstab Janke was alerted and told of Schmid's strong hunch. Frankfurt . . . Würzburg . . . Mannheim . . . Karlsruhe . . . Stuttgart . . . Any one of these cities could, Schmid thought, be the objective on the course now being flown by the heavy bombers of the R.A.F. He no longer felt that there might be a sudden veer to the east. But in the meantime, the single-engined night-fighters were rapidly exhausting their fuel as the lights and arrows tracing the invaders' course on the master-controller's map moved deeper and deeper into Germany.

Janke surveyed the battle-situation map in front of him and noted that the night-fighters of the 3rd Jagddivision at Deelen, under the command of General-Major Walter Grabmann, were airborne over radio-beacon Ida, south of Aachen; and the groups of the 1st Jagddivision at Döberitz, under the command of Oberst Hajo Herrmann, were in orbit round radio-beacon Otto, east of Frankfurt. Also above Otto were the squadrons of General-Major Max Ibel, who commanded the 2nd Jagddivision at Stade.

Janke was pleased to observe that the leading British formations were flying directly into the fighter boxes of the 5th Jagddivision in eastern France and the 1st Jagddivision in

Belgium and Holland. It would give the squadrons in those divisions an early opportunity to intercept and allow the sluicing-in of No. 1, 4 and 5 Squadrons before they were taken over for direction by the 7th Jagddivision.

As the Pathfinders which formed the spearhead of Harris's fleet neared the middle of the western frontier of Germany, all the German twin-engined night-fighters were in the air. Ju.88s of the 3rd Jagddivision, having taken off from Twente and Quakenbrück and set course for radio-beacon Ida, were vectored towards the bombers within minutes. Other Ju.88s from Langendiebach and Langensalza sped towards Ida and were fed into the bomber stream south and east of their airfields.

The veteran Me.110 groups from Venlo and Mainz-Finthen, attached to the crack 1st Fighter Corps of Night-Fighter Group 6 of the 7th Jagddivision, roared down their runways at one-minute intervals to keep a rendezvous above Ida; and Me.110s from St. Trond, already in the air north-east of Charleroi, were ordered to assemble over radio-beacon Bazi, almost directly north of their base. Soon they would be homed on to the bombers by signals flashed to them from beacon Murmeltier, south of Ida.

Night-fighters from the 2nd Jagddivision – stationed at Westerland, Stade and Vechta – were despatched to beacon Otto via beacon Ludwig, just north of Osnabrück, to close with the bombers north-east of Giessen. And aircraft from the 1st Jagddivision – based at Erfurt, Parchim, Stendal and Werneuchen – converged on Otto to be re-routed to Ida and unleashed into the stream. They were supported by single-engined fighters from the 1st, 2nd and 3rd Jagd-division, most of them arrowing through the night to radio-beacon Nordpol – one of the main assembly points for the fighters that defended Berlin. It was a long flight and many of them would soon have to land to refuel.

The war diary of General Schmid's 1st Jagdkorps shows that the total number of German aircraft committed to the action was two hundred and forty-six. And among the first of them to achieve 'kills' were the Me.110s from Loan-Athies in France and those from Mainz-Finthen, east of Frankfurt.

From the French field came a famous ace who was due for a busy and successful night – Oberleutnant Martin Drewes, commanding III Group of No. 1 Fighter Squadron, who lifted his Me.110 from the runway at Loan-Athies shortly after 2300 hours and pointed its nose across Belgium towards radio-beacon Ida. Huddled back-to-back behind twenty-six-year-old Drewes were his twenty-four-year-old radar operator, Oberfeldwebel Erich Handke, and air-gunner Oberfeldwebel Georg Petz. In front of Petz's knees were two 2cm drum-fed cannon, each of which held seventy-five rounds of ammunition. The guns, built-in at the back of the Messerschmitt's cabin, were aligned to shoot vertically at an elevation of between eighty and eighty-five degrees, and they were new to the aircraft.

Hitherto, Me.110s had been armed with two 3cm cannon – notable mainly for their tendency to jam. When they did fire, their muzzle-glare would temporarily blind the pilot; and their explosive power was so great that debris from a victim bomber would frequently endanger the attacker. The new vertical cannon minimised that risk, had a low consumption rate, and enabled the pilot to attack from below and to the side of a bomber – a position from which he could seldom be seen by his adversary. It was a distinct advantage; and highly skilled night-fighter pilots such as Drewes reckoned that with a drum of seventy-five rounds they could bring down five aircraft before having to reload.

Petz, sitting in the gunner's glasshouse common to Me.110s, had the basic job of scanning the sky behind and above for signs of a sudden attack. This, experience had taught night-fighter crews, was the air-space from which the R.A.F.'s long-range intruder Mosquitos would be most likely to swoop on them. He had at his disposal a twin-barrelled heavy machine-gun, but in action against a bomber his primary task would be to remove empty ammunition drums and clear jams.

Drewes, as soon as he was guided to a bomber by his radar operator, would – like other Me.110 pilots – visually aim through a special reflex sight fixed just above his head. And with an operator as experienced as Handke there would be many opportunities to use it. Before teaming up with Drewes, Handke had flushed out close on twenty bombers for other pilots to shoot down. With Drewes, he was to share in something like thirty-eight more victories.

"It was always a sinister feeling to hang only thirty to fifty metres under a Lancaster, always expecting fireworks: but nothing of the kind ever happened," Handke has since explained. "I always navigated my pilot to approximately two hundred metres below the enemy aircraft. When about fifty metres below the bomber's port wing we opened fire, aiming between the two engines into the fuel tanks; and then we dived directly to port to make sure the burning aircraft did not hit us. With this kind of attack we always shot first, where in theory the tail-gunner should have spotted us first."

This tactic was to reap its reward in burning bombers long before Harris's heavies could complete the dead-straight run to their turning point at Fulda.

Chapter Eight

The first night-fighter kills blazed in the Lüttich-Bonn-Koblenz area, and they marked for other searching fighters the course the British force was flying. But it was by sheer chance that Georg Petz saw his first bomber when Oberleutnant Drewes, under the direction of ground control, swung on to an easterly course. He was peering into the blackness around him when he suddenly glimpsed a four-engined aircraft almost directly over them. "Bomber above!" he yelled through the intercom. But the speeds of both aircraft were such that the bomber had streaked into the night even before it could be identified as either a Lancaster or a Halifax.

"Not to worry," Drewes said reassuringly as he banked the Messerschmitt into a steep climbing turn to port. "Where there is one there will be others."

When Drewes had levelled out on the easterly course, Handke switched on his Lichtenstein SN2 radar set and waited impatiently for the two cathode screens – one giving the height and the other the bearing of the target – to warm into a pale greenish glow. Then he deftly adjusted the brilliance . . . and immediately three blips were clearly pinpointed. From their size, they were unmistakably hostile aircraft. One of them he visually spotted in front of them and a little above the height at which they were flying.

Drewes eased back the throttles and was just able to make out four fingers of reddish-yellow light – the bomber's exhaust flames. Seconds later he saw the dark outline of a

Lancaster silhouetted in the moonlight. Handke, having picked it up on his screen, read out the target distance: "Six hundred metres . . . five hundred and fifty . . . five hundred . . ." Then he broke off. The SN2 could bring a night-fighter within five hundred metres of the target, but after that it could vector no further. This set had done its job. The rest was up to Drewes, who positioned the Messerschmitt below and to the port of the bomber and adjusted his speed to that of the Lancaster.

Unsuspectingly, the bomber flew on without even the usual gentle weave from port to starboard that gave its gunners a good chance of searching the blind quarter below.

Drewes manoeuvred closer; and he and his two crew members fixed their eyes steadily on the huge shape above them, chilled by the knowledge that a burst into the bomber's belly now would blow up its load – and them with it. But there was going to be nothing precipitate about this. He trimmed the distance between them with care, until the Messerschmitt was to the rear of and about fifty metres below the bomber. The egg-shaped scanner of the Lancaster's ground-to-air H2S radar set was clearly visible to him now between the rear-turret and the giant wing: and still there were no signs that his aircraft had been seen.

Juggling with his control column, Drewes neatly aligned the bomber in his reflex sight. Then he pressed the button that triggered off the two 2cm cannon, the Messerschmitt shuddering as they released their devastating fire.

Flames lanced along from the port inner engine of the Lancaster and licked across the wing: and a bloom of fire blossomed from the port outer engine.

Drewes thrust on full left rudder and threw the Me.110 into a blood-curdling, diving turn to port. And in those few seconds the Messerschmitt's crew saw the Lancaster fly on with flames spreading rapidly along its fuselage. Slowly its nose dipped, and the bomber slid into a zig-zag glide as the fire swept towards its tail. When it exploded in the air, east of Aachen, Drewes knew for certain that it still had its bomb-load aboard.

Levelling the Messerschmitt out, he pointed its nose upwards and set course for the east – where balls of fire in the sky ahead showed that other night-fighters had made contact with the bomber stream.

They had been flying for ten minutes on a heading of 100° when Handke saw another Lancaster flying above them and on the same course.

"We got fifty metres under it again," he recalls, "but the cannon jammed after the second shot and could not be reloaded. The Lancaster must have been hit, however, as she lost height quickly. But as we kept behind it, not having turned off in time, it must have spotted us, for suddenly it twisted into a corkscrew. We also dropped six hundred metres. At five hundred and fifty metres the Lancaster seemed to steady, and we had to overcome the compulsion to attack in our old way – where one was exposed to the fire of the tail-gunner. But we were already well used to the new tactics of firing into the wings, which did not endanger us so much when the bomber's load went off.

"At long last, Drewes raised the nose of our fighter and fired a long burst with his front armament into the bomber's starboard wing, which burst into flame. For a second or so he forgot to dive away, but there was no return fire from the rear-turret. The Lancaster's starboard inner engine dragged a banner of flame and its nose fell.

"As Drewes pulled away the Lancaster blew up, showering the sky with thousands of fiery fragments. I took a quick fix on my directional-finding gear and noted that the bomber had exploded in the air over the Vogelsberg area. Around us, bombers were dropping like flies sprayed with an insecticide gun.

"After a while, I spotted another bomber and navigated towards it. At seven hundred metres we could see it was another Lancaster. We were about to attack from the rear again when Petz, our air-gunner, announced that he had cleared the stoppage in our cannon. With the oblique cannon working we could now attack from below and to the side of the bomber, with less risk of being seen.

"Drewes edged the night-fighter closer, and for a few seconds we were almost on parallel course. Unaware, the Lancaster flew on. Then Drewes raked it with a long burst aimed into the wing. Flames fanned from the engines along the fuselage to acknowledge the accuracy of his shooting."

For a fleeting moment the crew of the Messerschmitt caught a glimpse of two men jumping from the stricken bomber, their bodies jack-knifing shut and turning over as they hurtled earthwards. Small puppet-like shapes, they were soon lost to sight, leaving the watchers to wonder whether their parachutes would open . . . if they had had time to clip them on.

By means of his radio-directional set, Handke was able to record the impact of the crashed Lancaster as approximately twenty kilometres north of Bamberg; and thinking about it, he marvelled again at the fact that the British bombers lacked a belly turret, without which they were an easy prey for the new oblique guns of the German fighters. He wondered, too, why the British had come on such a night. The weather was excellent for night-fighting: clear sky, moon, no clouds, no mist, and almost too much light.

Indeed, under a tent of stars the sickle moon shone brightly -- and the light-grey condensation trails left by the four-engined bombers stood out in sharp relief. Bursts of tracer fire gashed a night sky that was becoming lighter all the time. And below there was a ragged line of burning shot-down bombers that stretched as far as the eye could see.

Staffelkapitan Martin Becker of I/NJG 6, No. 1 Group, saw the black shape of a Halifax sliding beneath him and sent his Messerschmitt diving straight after it. Undetected by the bomber's air-gunner, he turned towards it and shot twice in rapid succession. The Halifax reared up and climbed at a crazy angle for a few seconds and then slipped into a wild glide before turning over, its fuselage a mass of flames.

While wireless-operator Karl Ludwig Johanssen was recording that the Halifax had hit the ground between Lüttich and north of Frankfurt at 0020 hours, Becker was already lining up his next victim. He had seen the silhouette of another four-engined aircraft three or four hundred metres away, and he was not going to waste time. Banking the Messerschmitt into attacking position, he kept the bomber in sight but for some quick glances in his immediate vicinity. It was clear of other aircraft, so he closed on the bomber – which he identified as a Halifax – fired at it and saw a flush of orange flame smear along its starboard wing. Another arm of fire reached from its outer engine as the Halifax tilted into a shallow corkscrew dive.

Becker swung the Messerschmitt round and, from close range, pumped another withering burst into the stricken British aircraft. The nose of the Halifax went down, and with awesome speed the plane hurtled almost vertically to the ground. Johanssen plotted its impact as being, again, between Lüttich and Frankfurt. The time was 0023 hours.

As the Messerschmitt crew looked down at the burning wreckage they saw six other bombers fall within seconds of each other – a proof of the success of fellow night-fighters nearby.

Ten minutes later, Becker sighted a Lancaster. With the confidence born of two rapid kills, he lined up on it and slanted his fire into its wing, drawing from it a stream of flame. The Lancaster pitched earthwards and detonated somewhere in the Lüttich area, which was fast becoming a graveyard for four-engined aircraft.

Two minutes later another Halifax fell to Becker's guns; and five minutes after that he brought down yet another.

The Messerschmitt had been in the air for some time now, and Becker knew that he would soon have to call a temporary halt. Checking his fuel gauges, he found that he had enough petrol left to keep him airborne for one more kill – but it would have to be a quick one. Not that he anticipated any difficulty there. The tell-tale lines of tracer now criss-crossing the night sky showed that combats were going on all around them. There were possible victims in plenty. And the string after string of close-knit explosions, confirming the deadly accuracy of the night-fighter interceptions and the terrible toll they were taking, made assurance doubly sure.

It was therefore no surprise when Johanssen picked up a blip on his radar screen almost at once and quickly guided Becker to the plane it represented: another Halifax. Becker framed it in his sights and gave it a five-second burst. The great coffin-shaped wing wheeled up and tilted over as the crippled Halifax reeled from the bomber pack. Johanssen logged its time of impact on the ground as 0050 hours.

Becker then swung his Messerschmitt in a wide circle and set course for base. But he was not finished with the night's game. Refuelled and with fresh ammunition for his guns, he later took off to intercept the bombers on their return trip, notching up his seventh victory that night with another Halifax which crashed south of Luxembourg at 0315 hours.

Now an agent for a car company in Wiesbaden, Becker says of his interceptions on the night of the Nuremberg raid, "There is not much to tell. There were such a lot of British bombers around that we could have knocked them down with a fly-flap."

Chapter Nine

At the controls of Pathfinder Lancaster S-Sugar, in the first
wave of the bomber stream, Wing Commander Daniels
had just made the course change at Charleroi when he saw
in the sky before him a brilliant orange-coloured flash.
Tracer hosed across somewhere to his port, and then
another dazzling splash of fire split the darkness nearby.
Moments later there was an explosion, followed quickly by
another.

Daniels switched on his intercom and said, "Skipper to
navigator. Log on the chart two bombers going down in
quick succession." He then warned his gunners to keep a
sharp look-out, telling them that as there was no flak to be
seen the bombers must have been shot down by fighters.

His instructions were received in silence. The crew of
S-Sugar shared a single ominous thought: they still had a
long way to go, and yet the German night-fighters were
already among them.

As for Daniels, the disquiet he had been feeling since first
seeing the flight plan for this raid increased as he observed
more bombers falling. But he stifled his unease and calmly
dictated the details to his navigator – the custom being for
bomber navigators to record on their charts the time and
place where aircraft were seen to go down during a raid and
also keep a tally of the number of men seen to escape by
parachute. Tonight, Daniels thought grimly as he gave the
information, there would be so many bomber casualties
that it would be hopeless to try to log them all. The time
would be better spent in trying to elude night-fighters.

Even as he came to this decision, a rainbow arc of fire

bathed the night some four hundred metres ahead. He reported it but this time told his navigator that it would be their last shoot-down entry, adding, "They'll know without us having to tell them how many have got the chop tonight."

More bombers were exploding to the right and left of them, showering the sky with flaming fingers of debris. It was not an encouraging sight for men committed to a course of action and Daniels dragged his eyes from it, telling his gunners to ignore shoot-downs and concentrate instead on their dark side – from which an attack would be most likely to come. He had another worry now, realising that his Lancaster was being clearly silhouetted against the burning and exploding bombers around him. It called for some sort of action. He called up his navigator and warned him that he was going to weave the aircraft a little in order to give the gunners a wider search area. Bomber Command discouraged this tactic on the grounds that it was likely to upset the accurate navigation so essential to a Pathfinder, as Daniels well knew. But on this occasion he considered that the large number of aircraft going down justified his decision.

As if to confirm his reasoning, long lines of tracer suddenly snaked to his starboard and criss-crossed with the more powerful trace of night-fighter cannon fire. Another combat was on. And it ended as abruptly as it had begun. Fire curled from the engine cowling of a bomber on their starboard and, fanned by the high wind and the slipstream from other aircraft, leapt along its wing and fuselage. Its fuel tanks blew up within seconds, and almost immediately afterwards there was a violent explosion as the bomb-load erupted.

Daniels tightened his grip on the control column of S-Sugar in readiness to throw the plane into an evasive corkscrew, regretting that he was flying with a new crew – men with whom he had never before flown; men whose reaction to danger was unknown to him. But that, he knew, was one of the handicaps of being the commanding officer of a squadron. He had to change crews periodically in order to give the benefit of his experience to fledglings. On a raid such as this was turning out to be, however, it would have been more reassuring to have had with him a crew he knew and could trust. No wonder most commanding officers did little operational flying, he reflected.

It had to be said for them, though, that the men he had with him now showed no signs of panic. Quietly and methodically, each of them was carrying out his job; and Daniels felt that they were going to be a good crew.

He glanced ahead and saw flares of a type he had never before seen floating down. They fell in fiery triangles and burst into brilliant pools of light, lazily illuminating the broad avenue formed by the bomber stream. At first they drifted in twos and threes. Then they seemed to shower down, wiping away what little cover of darkness had been left to shield the invading force. And by their light he saw the blazing outline of yet another Halifax as it plunged earthwards.

Knitted among the flares were odd and frightening clusters of fire that erupted in cascades of red-yellow sprays, looking very much like exploding bombers. But on careful scrutiny Daniels identified them as some kind of scarecrow rocket obviously intended to demoralise British crews by giving the impression that they were aircraft disintegrating. Pretty effective too, he thought – but surely unnecessary on this particular night. He hardly needed such spoofs to unnerve him when he'd already seen so many bombers going down for real – fifteen or sixteen at the very least.

Daniels' assessment of the losses so far was fairly accurate. In the fifteen minutes or so after the bombers had altered course at Charleroi for the straight four-hundred-kilometre run to Fulda – their final turning point – Bomber Command had lost about twenty aircraft.

Flying close behind Daniels was his flight-commander, Squadron Leader Keith Creswell, in another marker aircraft – Lancaster B-Beer. And he too was shocked by the number of flaming bombers he saw dropping from the sky. It didn't make him feel any happier, either, to note that the bright sickle moon was being reflected by a carpet of cloud directly beneath him, nakedly revealing his Lancaster to all comers. "One would have been less embarrassed in Piccadilly Circus with one's trousers down," he has since written. "The route was marked by burning or exploding aircraft, and for the first time I was aware that great losses were taking place. I remember considering that my chances of returning were slim."

Another Lancaster pilot was to say, "As I looked down from my bomber, I could see the vapour trails of about a score of other bombers lying below me. That was the sort of night it was. Not only was there a moon to help the enemy, but also their pilots could occasionally track us down from our vapour trails. We knew then that we would have to blast our way through to Nuremberg. All this was fairly early in the flight. Then to our port we saw our first combat. Tracer darted across the sky and an aircraft began to glow red in the night. Down it went in flames, and my mid-upper gunner was sure that it was a fighter.

"Most of the fighters seemed to have been waiting for us on the outskirts of the Ruhr, and it was here the battle began in earnest. While enemy searchlights raced across the gaps in the cloud in the hope of picking up any bomber that might have strayed off course, the fighters flew in to the attack.

"We found that they had already started dropping their flares, most of which were going down in clusters of three; and the fighters were laying them as close to our route as they possibly could. It wasn't safe to relax for a single moment."

This anonymous eye-witness report of the raid was broadcast in the Air Ministry Bulletin No. 13449 on 31st March 1944. And the same bulletin quoted Pilot Officer J.

Howell of Hobart, Tasmania, as saying, "We could see combats going on all round us. We spotted a single-seater FW.190 on our port side. It started to turn in underneath us, but our mid-upper gunner had it well covered as it made a diving turn. Then the fighter tried again from the other side, but before it could make the attack we cork-screwed into it and gave it the slip."

The bulletin goes on to quote Flight Sergeant R. Whinfield of Newcastle-upon-Tyne, on his thirteenth trip as a Lancaster pilot. Like Daniels, Whinfield was fascinated by the scarecrow rockets, of which he said, "They came up like flares and hung in the sky. Then they burst and scattered on the ground, like clusters of incendiaries. The explosion of one of them as it hit the ground looked almost as if a one-thousand-pounder was going off. There was just one damned thing after another, all the way to the target and on the journey home. Tracer showed that air combats were going on all the time and still more lights of various colours were being shot up as signals from enemy airfields as we passed overhead."

To make the inferno through which the British planes were flying even more hellish, the heavy anti-aircraft batteries of the massive Ruhr defences suddenly joined in the action. As far as the bombers were concerned, they could not have entered the battle at a worse time – for the changeable and incredibly strong March winds were playing havoc with the navigation of the less experienced crews, who found themselves strewn out in a broad lane well north of their flight course. The new German radar easily penetrated the widespread 'window' screen they had been dropping, and the anti-aircraft range-finders had little trouble in picking up these stragglers and sending heavy-calibre shells crashing among them.

Never had the ground defences known such a night. Usually, in their clashes with Harris's heavies, the gunners had only a few minutes in which to throw up their barrage before the tight pack of bombers flew out of their sector;

and if they were able to bring down one or two they had reason to feel wildly elated. But this time it was different. Lancasters and Halifaxes droned across their sights for nearly an hour, and they fell one after another to the unerring accuracy of predicted gunfire.

The sad truth was that many of these losses were really due to the failure of British crews to appreciate the fantastically high speed of the wind, which made a mockery of their navigation plots and led them into errors for which they paid with their lives.

Aircrews of the main-force No. 103 Squadron of Lancasters had been told before taking off from their base at Elsham Wolds, Lincolnshire, that the raid "should be a milk-run". They had also been assured by their Met officers that cloud and fog would completely black-out the Continent and that they could therefore expect practically no night-fighter opposition for some time after they had crossed the enemy coast.

The same was understood by their sister squadron, No. 576, flying with them from Elsham Wolds. Both squadrons were in the leading wave of the main force, tracking close behind the Pathfinders, and both were on 'maximum effort' – each putting up twenty-four aircraft.

At first there was no reason to doubt what the experts had told them, flying as they were in eight-tenths cloud until they crossed the coast. But then, to their utter dismay, they found that the sky was so clear that they could easily distinguish Halifaxes from Lancasters in the moonlight.

Among the Lancasters of No. 103 Squadron was D-Don of A Flight, loaded with a 4000lb 'cookie' and cans of incendiaries and captained by thirty-two-year-old Flying Officer Leonard Young – now a customs officer but then a post-officer clerk from Hull – with a crew drawn from both ends of the age scale. The navigator, Warrant Officer Alfred Shields, a clerk from Finchley in North London, was thirty years old, as was the bomb-aimer – Flight Sergeant George

Hatherway, a motor mechanic from Hurdley, Birmingham. But the mid-upper gunner – Paul Hawthorn of Hendon, Middlesex, who had just earned his sergeant stripes after joining the R.A.F. direct from school – was only eighteen; and the rear-gunner was another eighteen-year-old – Sergeant Clem Storey of Southend, who now owns his family's bookshop in Charing Cross Road, London. The wireless-operator was nineteen-year-old Sergeant Ronald Gardner of Tooting, London, also fresh from school. This was their nineteenth operation, ten of the previous ones having been against Berlin.

Shortly after leaving the coast, wireless-operator Gardner picked up on his Fishpond set some blips which looked suspiciously like those made by night-fighters and warned the gunners that one blip was astern and the other was in the upper port quarter.

Sergeant Storey, guided by directions from Fishpond, was the first to sight a fighter coming in. A staccato shudder rattled along the fuselage as he opened up with his four Brownings, and a few seconds later a new vibration shook the Lancaster as Sergeant Hawthorn brought the mid-upper turret into action.

With the sickly smell of cordite fumes seeping into his oxygen mask, Flying Officer Young shoved forward his control column, jammed on full left rudder and threw the Lancaster into a corkscrew to port. And not a moment too soon. Bursts of cannon fire and heavy machine-gun trace flashed above, missing them by seconds.

Storey reported that they had lost the fighter, and Young levelled out of the corkscrew – at which point Warrant Officer Shields groped under his chart table for the navigation instruments, which had been scattered when the bomber plunged into its wild dive. Hardly had he retrieved them when there was an almost simultaneous shout of "Corkscrew star'd, *go!*" from the gunners.

Young kicked on full right rudder and slammed the control column forward, throwing the bomber into a steep diving turn to starboard as enemy tracer shells zipped over their port wing. The eight Brownings chattered in challenge, and again the fuselage reeked of cordite.

Beads of cold sweat prickled Young's brow as he brought the Lancaster out of its dive and glanced at the altimeter. Precious height had been lost through the violent evasive action he had just taken, and something had to be done about it quickly; but first he had to know if they were still under attack.

Checking with the gunners, he learned that the enemy fighter had been an Me.110 and it had now disappeared. He therefore swung the Lancaster back on course and began to climb, the plane's 5000h.p. engines whining into a new note as he opened the throttles for more power. The aircraft was responding well, and from the feel of the controls he was certain that if they had suffered any damage it could only be slight. He was more concerned about the crew and was relieved to discover that no one had been wounded in the two attacks.

Ahead of them a fiery cross glowed in the sky, etching out the lines of a Lancaster; and over to their port a ribbon of flame trailed across the darkness. Two more bombers – two more crews – had done their last op. And the veterans of D-Don watched for a moment, appalled by the frightening suddenness of death all around them and their own near miss. They saw both of the stricken aircraft rise almost vertically and then turn over on their backs to plunge to earth in twin arcs of fire. It was a moment of drama, translated into one bleak sentence in D-Don's log-book: "One Lancaster and one other unidentified bomber downed by fighters east of Aachen."

The force of which they were a part had a long way to go, but already the entire German night-fighter strength seemed to be up there among them – winged sentinels of death, marking their course with flaming crosses. But for the vigilance of the gunners, D-Don could well have been one of those blazing crosses. Might still be. The silent crew had no illusions about that. Within the next few heartbeats someone out in that petrified sky could be entering *them* in a log-book. "One Lancaster . . ."

Flight Sergeant Gardner, now a fire-brigade officer in Kenley, Surrey, recalls, "The fighters were waiting for us shortly after we crossed the coast, as if they already knew our target and route. And they were in force. Never have I seen so many gathered at one point during my tour of operations. We were attacked about three or four times, but as soon as the fighters realised by our evasive action that we were alert they seemed to sheer off to look for less vigilant crews.

"Everything was fine until we left the coast. The clouds we had been flying in suddenly broke and the sky was absolutely clear . . . and it was full of Me.109s and 110s. Twice we were attacked by a pair of 109s. But as soon as they realised we had seen them they broke contact. Normally, flying in the leading wave, we were seldom attacked by fighters until well into France or Germany. This raid was the only one in thirty operations when I could see in large numbers our fellow bombers. I counted fifteen of them being shot down within fifteen minutes of crossing the enemy coast.

"The losses, I think, were increased by pilots ramming their throttles through the gate to get more speed and burning their exhaust stubs off. Then they were lit up like Christmas trees and easy targets.

"Usually the fighters took at least half an hour to get amongst us. But this time they seemed to be waiting in strength . . ."

Chapter Ten

From all over Germany the single-engined and twin-engined night-fighters poured towards the radio-beacons of the Ruhr defences. In the first wave were the Ju.88s of the crack 3rd Jagddivision commanded by General Grabmann at Deelen. The second group of NJG 2, equipped with the newer and faster Ju.88 R2, scrambled from Quakenbrück at 2341 hours with orders to patrol west of the Ruhr on a southerly heading.

When almost at Aachen, one of the Ju.88s from Quakenbrück – piloted by Oberleutnant Koeberich, with Oberfeldwebel Walter Heidenreich as wireless-operator and Oberfeldwebel Kramell as air-gunner – picked up on its radar an enemy contact some five kilometres away. The Oberleutnant skidded the plane into a tight turn to port, levelled out and flew parallel with the Rhine on a south-easterly course, maintaining height at around 5000 metres.

Heidenreich adjusted the brilliance of his radar screen and then peered closely at it in surprise. The blip he was tracking had an extraordinary look about it. He had never seen one quite like it before. What was even more puzzling was that it was moving at a fantastically high speed for an enemy bomber, quite apart from the fact that it was a much bigger blip than that normally thrown up by a Lancaster or a Halifax.

He called up his pilot and told him of this phenomenon. Oberleutnant Koeberich acknowledged the report and set his guns to visual firing. Meanwhile, Heidenreich continued to scrutinise the contact on his screen. On rare occasions he had picked up two British bombers flying in close formation, but seldom at night and then only for a few minutes. More often than not they were aircraft that had joined forces by chance in the hope that the combined effect of their armament would ward off attacks by night-fighters: but the strain on the aircraft, the throttles of which had to be juggled to keep them in formation – thus increasing their petrol consumption – was really too great to make the effort worthwhile.

Aware of all this but not entirely discounting the possibility, Heidenreich was even further surprised when the mysterious trace on his screen climbed sharply for long stretches of the hunt. And its speed was such that the Ju.88 had difficulty in keeping up with it.

Koeberich, fearing that he might lose whatever it was, rammed his throttles forward and gradually narrowed the gap. It was the first time he had flown the Mark R2, and he realised when he checked his air-speed that had they been in the previous version of the Ju.88 their quarry would easily have outflown them.

While vectoring the night-fighter metre by metre closer to the blip, Heidenreich took a fix and noted that they were now nearing Mainz at an altitude of 6700 metres. And at that moment there was a shout of "Lancaster! Lancaster!" from his two fellow crew-members. As Heidenreich had first suspected, their prey was in fact two Lancasters flying in tight formation, almost dead ahead and slightly above them. That they must be the pathfinders was taken for granted by the night-fighter.

Cautiously, Koeberich brought the Ju.88 under the Lancaster on his port side – which was a little ahead of the other – and tapped on port rudder. Then he carefully manoeuvred the night-fighter to within eight metres of the bomber and blasted it with his side cannon. As fire billowed from the bomber's wing, he flew crabwise under the second Lancaster and raked that too with his side cannon.

Says Heidenreich, "Blitz-fast there was a repetition of what had happened only a few seconds earlier. Now we saw two burning bombers flying side by side, still on their original course. We took up position three hundred metres to the starboard of them and flew a parallel course. Number One Lancaster dipped towards the left and Number Two to the right, to crash north and south of the Rhine with mighty explosions. Even at our height it was light as day for a second or so.

"We logged these shoot-downs at 0046 hours and 0047 hours. We did not notice any of the crews bale out, although to us there was plenty of time for them to have done so because our cone of fire went into the wings.

"The crash-points were visible visiting cards. Cascades of technicolored Christmas trees burned on the ground for a long time, showing beyond doubt that they were Pathfinders; and it was especially rewarding to have got a pair of them so quickly.

"We believed we had intercepted the spearhead of the enemy bomber formation, but despite intensive searching we did not pick up any other targets on our radar. In reality, we had caught two delayed Pathfinders."

With fuel running out, the Ju.88 landed in Kassel-Rothweston. It was to be the last operation for Koeberich's crew. (A week later, on 8th April – Easter Sunday – American Boeing squadrons attacked their base at Quakenbrück and laid seven carpets of bombs. Koeberich, who on 1st April had been promoted to captain of the 6th Echelon, was among the dead; and his flight mechanic air-gunner Kramell was wounded. Heidenreich, who had gone on leave an hour before the attack, returned to duty as the victims of the raid were being laid out in a long row in the marketplace of Quakenbrück to await burial.)

To combat the long-range intruder activities of the R.A.F.'s Night Striking Force of Mosquitos, the Germans had modified many of their twin-engined Me.110s and made them interceptors. This had been done by fitting extra fuel tanks to the aircraft and adding a rear-gunner to the hitherto two-man crew of pilot and radio-operator – the gunner controlling two movable heavy-calibre machine-guns.

With a speed of between 420 and 450 kilometres an hour near the ground, the Messerschmitt interceptor had excellent manoeuvrability and it performed well in climbing; but its efficiency was drastically limited in bad weather because the elevator and aileron controls had to be operated by a stick instead of a wheel. It therefore needed extremely competent airmen to fly it in inclement weather and during the night hours.

A group of such interceptors was I/NJG 3, stationed at Vechta and Wittmundhafen in northern Germany.

By the time this group was ordered to take off, at 2300 hours, the control staff of the German night-interception units had correctly distinguished the main-force bombers from the smaller groups of enemy aircraft that had for some time been flying minor harassing or feint attacks; and weather conditions were far better than had at first been anticipated.

Aircrews of I/NJG 3 had been ordered to fly to the radio-beacon at Frankfurt-am-Main, from where they would be fed into the bomber formation; and as they climbed to operating height, brisk voices from ground observation posts supplied them with the altitudes, speeds and headings of the bombers. But the course they had been given to fly to their radio assembly point was dead straight and therefore presented them with two hazards. One was that the long-range Mosquitos, with their efficient radar, would have little difficulty in detecting them and might try shooting them down; and the other was that with so many aircraft already orbiting the beacon there would be the danger of collisions.

Leutnant Hans Meissner – a twenty-five-year-old I/NJG 3 pilot with seventeen four-engined British bombers to his credit – decided to lessen these risks by steering a course which, he estimated, would take him more quickly to the spearhead of the enemy formation. The clouds which had been blanketing the southern region were breaking into vast caverns through which the moon shone brightly, and in such conditions he considered that he could rely on the visual sighting of targets.

Far ahead of him he could see the flak burst and splutter among the groping arms of the searchlights, and every now and then there was a brilliant glow in the sky, barely there for a moment before exploding into nothingness. Thin, spidery multi-coloured threads wove a crazy patchwork pattern in the darkness as combats began and as quickly ended.

Meissner looked at the luminous hands of the clock set in his dashboard and saw that it was exactly twenty-nine minutes after midnight – 0029 hours. One minute later his radar operator announced that he had a contact on his screen.

Flying on the bearing he was given, Meissner visually picked up the exhaust fires of a four-engined bomber north-west of Frankfurt. He edged closer and identified it as a Lancaster, its black under-surface clearly silhouetted against the moonlight. And almost immediately his radar operator made another contact. The second bomber was also a Lancaster, and Meissner spotted it about a thousand metres ahead. He mentally noted its position and then concentrated on the first one.

Easing back his control column, he brought the snub-nosed Messerschmitt up in a gentle climb and trained his fixed forward guns on the starboard inner engines of the bomber, prepared for it to go into a steep evasive dive to port as soon as he attacked.

From a distance of 150 metres, and fifty metres below the Lancaster, Meissner opened fire. Flames flicking along the bomber's starboard wing confirmed his hit. He pushed the stick forward and slapped on left rudder as four streams of tracer hosed from the rear-turret of the stricken aircraft to whip past somewhere to his port. His steep turn to port brought the burning bomber once again into his sights, but he was now ready for another kill.

The second Lancaster, alerted by the attack, began to take desperate evasive action; but the Messerschmitt doggedly went after it, Meissner keeping the bomber in his sights. Its pilot, his bomb-load still aboard, tried a last, frantic manoeuvre to lose his stalker by spinning his aircraft into a corkscrew dive.

Meissner remembers, "As the great port wing of the Lancaster came upright as the pilot whipped it into a right-hand dive, I rolled over on my back and shot him down virtually from above. Since the wing tanks were unprotected on the upper side by armoured plate, the effect of my fire was devastating."

The times of these two kills were recorded in Meissner's log-book as 0031 hours and 0037 hours, both north-west of Frankfurt-am-Main.

Of the combats which raged along the skyway between Frankfurt and Nuremberg, Meissner says, "All hell was let loose for the enemy . . . Burning aircraft made the night even brighter than it was before."

After shooting down the second Lancaster – bringing his total score of confirmed kills to twenty-one – he found that his instruments had become unserviceable, and so he set course for base. But there was more to it than that. The intense strain of continual night-fighting was having its effect on Meissner. With the sincerity and honesty that marks a man as a true fighter rather than a braggart, he now frankly admits, "Because of the excellent visibility it would have been possible to continue flying, but I broke off the flight because I was nervous at the end."

Among the Me.110s which had taken off from Vechta was the 3rd Echelon of I/NJG 3, with one of Germany's crack night-fighter pilots at the controls of Me.110-G4. Oberfeld-webel Rudolf Frank was on his 176th night-fighter opera-tion, and with him was his radar/wireless-operator Oberfeldwebel Hans Georg Schierholz; but his usual air-gunner, Sergeant Heinz Schneider, had been stood-down so that a young pilot freshly arrived from night-fighter training could be taken up for first-hand instruction.

A few minutes after lifting from the runway at Vechta, Schierholz received an order from ground control for his pilot to fly to radio-beacon Ludwig, a few miles north of Osnabrück; and as the Messerschmitt climbed to operating height, he tuned in to the frequency of the Divisional Battle Headquarters at Stade, near Hamburg, and had his position fixed by directional finder.

The pre-flight instruction had been that their tactic for the night would be Zahme Sau (wild boar) – the code-name for a manoeuvre in which three or four night-fighters flew in close formation and were then sluiced simultaneously into the enemy bomber stream by ground control. But at the Stade headquarters they had now assessed the actual course of the British bomber force, which had been flying dead straight ever since leaving Charleroi; and earlier shoot-downs had confirmed to the controllers that Harris's heavies were not jinking or dog-legging in any way. The Zahme Sau order to the interceptors from Vechta was therefore countermanded almost as soon as it had been given. Instead, G4 was instructed to speed with throttles wide open in a south-easterly direction on a course estimated to take it among the vanguard of the leading bombers.

Frank and Schierholz had the best records in their echelon, and it had been decided before take-off that they should broadcast any course changes they might have to make to the other fighters in their group. This they now did by transmitting a signal over their trailing aerial – with highly successful results: for when G4 made contact with the bombers it was in the company of the whole echelon.

"After we had flown for about ten minutes in a southerly direction," Schierholz recalls, "we received the message from divisional headquarters that the enemy were flying on an easterly course between Köln and Coblenz. We confirmed this by our own observation, for we could see three or four aircraft crashing ahead of us. On this heading we could theoretically cross the course of the in-flying bombers – and that was what happened. I picked up an enemy contact on my radar, and when we got to within two kilometres we swung on to the same course and placed ourselves about three hundred metres beneath it. From this position we could quickly get at it. Gradually we worked ourselves to about fifty to a hundred metres on the dark side of the bomber where, with the lighter sky behind it, we were able to see it more clearly.

"The great shape of a Lancaster loomed before us. We manoeuvred until we were right under it and climbed on a matching course to within a hundred metres. The Lancaster had still not seen us and flew calmly on its way. My pilot aimed at the wing, between the fuselage and the inner engine, and fired with his two oblique-mounted two-centimetre cannon. One burst set the fuel tanks ablaze. We usually aimed the burst slightly in front of the wing, and by lightly pulling up the nose of the Messerschmitt we ensured that the bomber flew through our cone of fire.

"When it was clear that the fire could not be controlled, we turned downwards to starboard. We went starboard because in our experience most pilots confronted with sudden danger dived towards port. The burning bomber hit the ground at 0001 hours in the region west of the Vogelberges. It was the fortieth night-fighter success of our crew."

On orders from their divisional headquarters, Frank and Schierholz stayed in the area of their kill and, ten minutes later, another contact appeared on their radar. They rapidly closed on it and found that it was a Lancaster, shooting it down with the same tactics they had used before. Their log-book recording showed that the burning bomber crashed at about 0018 hours in the region north of Fulda.

Messerschmitt G4 continued the hunt, and a third

bomber – this time a Halifax – fell to its guns. Schierholz recounts, "After about fifteen to twenty minutes further search, I got a new contact. I guided the pilot to visual range and we recognised a four-engined Handley-Page Halifax. On instructions from headquarters in Stade we flew for about five minutes with the bomber in order to enable its course and altitude to be plotted through our own d/f (direction-finding) signals, which were being noted by our ground d/f stations. After this information had been evaluated, we received permission to attack. We followed the same tactics as before and at about 0057 hours the Halifax crashed in flames in the region of the Rhön. We searched around for another target, but without success. Then we received the order to land at Langendieback, near Hanau, and get the aircraft ready to come into action immediately.

"Between fifty and sixty night-fighters had already landed there, and this led to a delay in refuelling. We therefore broke off the operation and flew back to Vechta as we knew we would not be able to catch up with the bombers."

Chapter Eleven

Lancaster H-Harry of No. 50 Squadron lurched and rolled in the slip-streams of the hundreds of bombers ahead and levelled out at an operating height of 19,000 feet at exactly 2300 hours. Behind it lay the enemy coast and a sky that was pockmarked with shells from the coastal defence batteries.

The Lancaster had notched up only a few miles when its crew saw the brilliant beams of searchlights sweeping the sky in wide arcs with an appearance of growing urgency. Interwoven among the great pyramids of light were ominous signs of the air-to-air combats that were taking place. Red and green tracer snaked across the backcloth of night; and dazzling mushrooms of fire hung for a moment, terrifyingly beautiful against the darkness, before trailing away to leave thousands of fiery splinters in their wake.

H-Harry droned on; and with each minute – or so it seemed to Sergeant Rowlinson, wireless- and radar-operator – more and more bomber shoot-downs were being logged. He had never actually seen an aircraft blasted out of existence, so he eventually decided to leave his compartment for a moment and satisfy his morbid but compulsive curiosity.

Hardly had he stepped into the astro-dome of the bomber than a pennant of flame unfurled in the sky ahead of him. Fascinated, he watched it bloom into a vivid orchid of fire before it slid earthwards. But the sudden horrifying realisation that this was death in the air – the ultimate penalty for the unwatchful – severely jolted him, and he hurriedly scrambled back to his compartment on the port side of the

75

aircraft and intently scanned his Fishpond screen with a heightened sense of alertness and responsibility.

His radar eye was a cathode-ray tube which had a small screen some eight inches in diameter. It picked up signals transmitted from a radio housed in the rear of the bomber – signals which, if they hit a solid object such as an aircraft, bounced back and showed on the screen as two tiny wavy lines. If the aircraft reflecting the signals came nearer, the blips would become correspondingly larger. Such a contact could be safely assumed to be an interceptor, and its direction and bearing could be estimated.

Rowlinson breathed heavily into his oxygen mask and heartily wished that H-Harry had never taken off from Skellingthorpe. Not for the first time, he cursed those who had decided to put off-leave crews on the operation . . . And then he had reason to think that if he had stayed another half-minute in the astro-dome H-Harry would soon be one of those flaming onions in the night – for a blip, small at first but rapidly growing in size, was there on his screen.

Urgently, he called up his pilot – Flight Lieutenant 'Chas' Startin, an Australian from Tarbinga, Queensland – to warn him that a fighter was approaching fast from four o'clock on their port quarter; and he was just receiving an acknowledgement when rear-gunner Sergeant Hopkinson shouted for them to corkscrew to port. Hopkinson could see the enemy plane clearly enough to identify it as an Me.110.

The blip made by the fighter now filled the Fishpond screen, and Rowlinson's body jerked with nervous reaction as the Lancaster's four rear Brownings chattered in harsh bursts. Seconds later, Sergeant Ernest McIlwaine – H-Harry's short and stocky mid-upper gunner – blasted off with his four Brownings.

Meanwhile, Startin was twisting and weaving the bomber to decrease the angle of the night-fighter's fire. But by now Hopkinson, looking out from his rear-turret, was able to inform Startin that the fighter, possibly hit, had broken off the attack.

The Flight Leiutenant brought the bomber back on course and warned his crew to keep a sharp look-out. He then asked his navigator, Pilot Officer T. Evans – a Canadian standing in for the regular navigator, who was on the sick list – to give him a new course to the target. While waiting for it, he trimmed the Lancaster and gradually began to claw back the height they had lost. But he was perturbed to see that the moon was getting brighter, and he again called up the crew to warn them that the operation would be almost like a daylight raid. Then he swung the Lancaster on to the new course that Evans had just given him.

At this point Rowlinson's Fishpond screen went completely blank. It could, he thought, have been damaged in the attack; but he also knew that the picture would fade if the rear escape-hatch accidentally opened and let in cold air to blow on the transmitter and cool the valves. This seemed a probable cause, under the circumstances, so he decided to go and check.

Disconnecting his oxygen mask from the main supply and clipping on his portable bottle he groped his way along the fuselage, but the weaving of the Lancaster made it heavy going and he rested for a moment under the mid-upper turret. The turret swivelled backwards and forwards as the gunner searched the sky in long sweeps; but Rowlinson was not concerned with that. From where he was, he could see that he had guessed right: the escape door was wide open. And he heaved a sigh of relief, because it meant that his Fishpond set was no doubt still serviceable.

Gingerly, he edged himself along the side of the fuselage, groping for hand-holds: and twice he tried to grasp the open door, missing it each time because the aircraft lurched.

It then struck him that he had left his parachute in his radio-compartment, not having considered the risk he would be taking if the door was open and he had to try to shut it against the pressure from the slip-stream of the engines. But he thought about it now. A sudden twist of the Lancaster and he could be sucked through the open hatch. It was not a pleasing prospect, and he started to sweat although the temperature outside was well below zero. Nevertheless, having come this far, he had no intention of going back without accomplishing what he knew had to be done.

On his next attempt he managed to grasp the door, and somehow – though to this day he is not sure how – he was just able to slam it shut. But the effort exhausted him and he had to rest for a moment before making the trip back to the nose of the aircraft.

When he reached his compartment he slumped into his seat, reconnected to the main supply and sucked in long gasps of oxygen as he gave his attention to the Fishpond set. There was no time for him to dwell on the chance he had just taken. Nuremberg had yet to be reached, and another night-fighter trace might come up at any moment on his radar. There was still a job to do.

Fishpond was to save the lives of many bomber crews that night by warning them in time of the night-fighters hunting them. Among the lucky ones was Flight Sergeant Ramsden, wireless-operator of Halifax M-Mother. A veteran of the Berlin raids, Nuremberg meant relatively little to him as a target. It was just another 'op'; and it was only in retrospect that it acquired special significance.

Ramsden had lost one crew early in 1943 and was no longer prepared to gamble on his chances of coming back – no matter what the target. Thus when the aircrews on his station were asked whether they wanted their one-egg ration before or after the trip, he had opted for his in advance. Only twenty years of age, he had already been recommended and accepted for a commission that had not yet come through; but although he had gone so far as to be measured for his officer's uniform he was not promising himself that he would ever get to wear it. There were many like him . . . not so much pessimistic as realistic, the casualty rate at the time being so high.

And it was not that Ramsden doubted the quality of the men with whom he was flying. His pilot, Squadron Leader Cooper, D.F.C., had completed one tour of operations; and only the tail-gunner was not a regular crew member. But Flight Lieutenant F. Taylor was the squadron's gunnery leader with no crew of his own, and he had stepped in when M-Mother's usual tail-gunner had reported sick. Ramsden had himself occasionally flown as a 'spare' when other crews had a regular member on the sick list, and he knew that most men tried to avoid it because it often meant going out with an inexperienced crew. Four of his own hut-mates had been stripped of their sergeant stripes for refusing to fly 'spare' with pilots who were not known to them; but he was certain that Flight Lieutenant Taylor had had no such qualms about joining this crew.

M-Mother had taken off from Breighton, Yorkshire, at 2200 hours and had flown above cloud until it reached the French coast. Loaded with four 1000lb high-explosive bombs, and with the usual cans of incendiaries in the wings, it was in the second wave of Harris's force.

Shortly after leaving the coast, it had become plain to the crew that the Met men had boobed badly. The sky was clear of cloud, and the moonlight was far too bright for a deep-penetration raid. Things couldn't have been more different from what they had been led to expect.

They were unperturbed by the light and heavy flak that was coming up from the ground defences, for they expected it and were used to it. But they were uneasily aware that the weather was very much in favour of the German night-fighters, whom they knew to be a far greater potential danger than anti-aircraft fire.

Like other navigators, M-Mother's had given up logging bombers seen to have been brought down; and for once

Ramsden had found it too unnerving for him to concentrate on his *Daily Mirror* crossword puzzle – crosswords having completely absorbed him during the early part of previous operations. Instead, he was finding out a little more about the Fishpond set that had been installed in the Halifax only that morning and on which he had been given a scant half-hour of tuition. It was just as well. The set had scarcely warmed up when a blip appeared on the screen, with a smaller blip circling it. Whatever the blips represented, he estimated that they were about five miles away.

Reporting this, he asked the gunners if they could see anything. But the distance was too great for visual confirmation and he had to content himself with watching them on his screen, in puzzlement, for the next ten minutes. Their behaviour was certainly intriguing. One kept on a fairly constant course, but the smaller one twisted and turned erratically. Then the larger of the blips began to act oddly and suddenly moved from the screen entirely.

Again Ramsden called the gunners, but this time he asked if they had seen anything that looked like an aircraft going down. Flight Lieutenant Taylor, from the rear-turret, confirmed that he had just seen a bomber going down in flames about four miles to their port quarter; and Ramsden, heartened because he was obviously reading the set with some accuracy, settled down to watch it even more closely than before.

The sickle moon was getting brighter, but below it was still pitch black; and every now and then, M-Mother's crew saw the shapes of bombers as they appeared in the lighter segments of the sky before flitting hurriedly on to seek the darkness. They looked like ghostly forms that were fleeing in fear from the similar wraiths around them – wraiths that might suddenly spit tracer at them, mistaking them for enemy fighters.

An unusual silence had settled over M-Mother's crew, but it was broken when Ramsden switched on his intercom and warned the gunners that he had picked up a suspicious contact almost dead astern. The blip loomed ever larger on his screen and was closing rapidly from a range of half a mile. He instructed the rear-gunner to line his guns ten degrees up in the port quarter and watch.

Taylor, checking his starboard quarter first, swung his turret to port and swiftly aligned the four Brownings at the angle given him by Ramsden, his gloved thumb resting lightly on the firing button.

Squadron Leader Cooper, meanwhile, kept the Halifax on course and made no attempt to weave or dive.

The wavy lines of the contact now embraced both sides of the Fishpond screen, indicating that a confrontation was imminent – and Ramsden began to sweat profusely. A shout from the gunnery leader that he could see the fighter somewhat relieved the tension: and an instant later there was the rattle of the four Brownings as Taylor directed a long point-blank burst at the enemy plane.

"He's on fire! Going down to port!" Taylor shouted.

Ramsden jerked back his blackout curtain and peered through the porthole in time to glimpse a single-engined FW.190 as it hurtled under their wing-tip in a mass of flames.

"This victory was confirmed, but the main victory was unquestionably Fishpond's," Ramsden wrote later. "The German pilot may not have seen us. If he did, he must have been plain green or plain mad to fly within three hundred yards of the rear-gunner. Another five seconds on that course and we could have thrown cream-puffs at him."

They logged the shoot-down and flew on without conversation, comforted by the monotonous but familiar throbbing of the Halifax's great radial engines.

It was almost midnight. Soon they should reach the final turning point at Fulda.

The crew of Y-Yorker, of No. 44 Squadron, sighted their first combats shortly after they made the change of course at Charleroi for the 250-mile leg to Fulda. They had just narrowly missed colliding with another bomber through dog-legging upon finding that the Met forecast of wind-speed was entirely wrong.

Their flight-engineer, Flight Lieutenant Burrows, recalls, "Things really began to happen then. Combats appeared to be going on all around us, with aircraft blowing up as they received direct hits. Some exploded so close to us that our Lancaster rocked alarmingly, as if every rivet would pop out from its socket. It was our duty to report each combat to the navigator, who logged the height, speed, time and position of it. But after the tenth was reported, our skipper – Wing Commander Thompson – told us to disregard them. The atmosphere was tense and I continued to report them. I was frightened out of my wits when the skipper dug me in the ribs and shouted, 'I said enough!' These conditions persevered for what seemed like ages. It was obvious to all of us that we were suffering alarming casualties with little or no cloud protection."

North of Frankfurt, Y-Yorker was caught by the searchlights. Two fastened on to it and held it relentlessly; then a third, like a vulture disputing a kill, swooped across the sky to lay its own claim to the Lancaster with a beam that blinded the crew.

Wing Commander Thompson felt both naked and helpless as he threw the bomber into a corkscrew that had it diving and twisting like a trapped animal fighting frantically for its life. The magnetic needle of the compass in front of him spun crazily as he pushed and pulled on the control column, his feet pressing hard on the rudder pedals, in a wild and desperate bid to escape from the imprisoning arms of light.

And the crew could do nothing. Eyes that had become accustomed to scanning layers of darkness were brutally assaulted by the dazzling glare that made the aircraft virtually a sitting target for the anti-aircraft guns below.

But the expected streams of flak, which would normally have been poured into the centre of the cones of light by now, were absent: and it took a moment or two for Y-

Yorker's crew to realise that the sky must be so full of night-fighters that the ground gunners dared not fire for fear of hitting their own aircraft. It was cold comfort. Soon, no doubt, one of those fighters would home in on their coning and blast them into eternity.

Thompson, with this in mind, made another frenzied effort to escape from the searchlights by rolling the Lancaster into a starboard dive. Then, when its port wing reared up, he pulled back hard on the control column – the blood draining from his head and his eyes blurring before he relaxed the pressure on the wheel and let the bomber slip into an uneven skid. When he looked down and behind, he saw the searchlights weaving frenziedly back and forth in what might have been baffled rage.

He called for a fresh course and began the slow job of getting back to his operating height, after which Y-Yorker flew on for an uninterrupted forty-five minutes. And with each air-mile the crew marvelled at the number of combats they saw, now and then catching clear glimpses of enemy fighters as they darted across the bomber stream.

They had just made the course alteration for Fulda when they were themselves attacked. Flight Sergeant Hall, in the rear-turret, was the first to see the FW.190 as it streaked in on them. He shouted for a corkscrew to starboard; and then, as the Lancaster ploughed downwards, he called for them to pull out of it fast.

The fighter followed them in a tight turn, but Hall was unable to bring his guns to bear on it because of the Lancaster's violent evasive twists. He called for another dive to port, and again the bomber plunged downwards. When he peered out through his turret the fighter had melted into the night, seeking a less watchful crew.

Thompson brought Y-Yorker back on course for Fulda.

Chapter Twelve

As more and more of the Luftwaffe's fighter force grappled with Harris's heavies, an order was sent out to the German ground gunners to restrict their fire. There was now a very real danger of them bringing down their own aircraft. Besides, there was no point in wasting ammunition: the night-fighters were doing all that was necessary. Those first interceptions had proved how ideal conditions were for the visual sighting and shooting down of bombers once they had been picked up by a fighter's radar . . . so let them get on with it.

But many of the German night-fighter crews had not anticipated such a night. Those of No. 8 Staffel of NJG 1, flying Me.110s, were surprised even to have been scrambled from their French base at Loan-Athies. To what purpose? they had asked themselves. The moonlight was surely far too bright for the British to risk a raid.

This consideration was uppermost in the mind of Oberleutnant Dieter Schmidt, Staffelkapitan of No. 8, as he led his Me.110s to radio-beacon Ida. He couldn't help thinking that it was a false alarm. That he quickly learned it wasn't is borne out by his impressions of the raid, written shortly after he landed. His report reads:

They come. Suddenly we are in the middle of them . . . course 120 to 150 degrees. Ack-ack fire . . . Recognition signal. One shot down! Another! All the time more of them. I see one right in front of me. With my second burst of fire all I get is a miserable 'bum-bum'. The guns have jammed. I turn off course, change the magazines, test them again. Some go off but two cannon are completely out of action.

My target has gone. Around us it is raining shot-down aircraft. Someone behind me. Swing away . . . to the right ack-ack is bursting furiously. All hell is let loose. Everywhere explosions and air-to-air trace. Everywhere aircraft and bombs falling . . . a night the like of which I have never known. 0045 hours, 5700 metres. Attention! One on the left, 300 to 200 metres. Colossally huge, it flashes by us and I almost ram him. We wheel to the right, pull up to him . . . 100 metres, he twists . . . even better target. I keep him just ahead, framed in my sights. Fire! He swings starboard and slides through my cone of fire. Immediately flames sweep along his fuselage and pour from his starboard inner engine.

That should be enough. I come right past him. See it's a Halifax. He shoots back. I pull away and see the cockade and the recognition marking NP. Then he is behind to the left, diving down. He hits the ground at 0049, somewhere about 50 to 100 km north-west of Würzburg . . . in the mountains. We've been hit in the port wing.

The then twenty-four-year-old Oberleutnant, now a doctor living in Hofheim (Taunus), was amazingly accurate in the split second in which he noted the Halifax's marking: the identification letters NP were those of No. 158 Squadron of Lisset in Yorkshire. And he was right, too, about being hit. For when he examined his Messerschmitt after landing at Langendiebach he found, to his horror, some human hair and flesh stuck to the port boss of the aircraft. Explains Dr. Schmidt, holder of the coveted Ritterkreuz with thirty-nine victories to his credit – the Halifax being his eighteenth, "We frequently found small parts of enemy aircraft in our fighters – pieces of perspex and metal – thrown out by the explosive power of our twenty-millimetre cannon. It is obvious that in the few seconds we took to down the

Halifax nobody in it was able to have the time to snap on a parachute and jump. So I can only attribute the fragments of hair and flesh to parts of the enemy air-gunner. This was the only time that we found parts of a human body on our Me.110. Usually we shot at the engines and the petrol tanks, for they burned easier and faster. But in this particular action I hit the body of the bomber."

Also surprised at being scrambled that night was Leutnant Wilhelm Seuss, the Me.110 pilot of IV/NJG 5 who had earlier decided that his coming leave would not be in jeopardy thanks to the moonlight. At 2300 hours he was disillusioned – and disappointed - for NJG 5 was at that time alerted that British formations were flying over in strength. And seventeen minutes later the Messerschmitts from Erfurt were roaring down the runway with orders to fly west. So much for the Leutnant's long-awaited leave.

At an altitude of 6000 metres the force levelled out in the neighbourhood of Frankfurt where, anxiously watching their fuel gauges, the pilots orbited for fifteen minutes. Then, at about 0015 hours, they noticed lights in the sky.

Looking back, Seuss – a doctor now living in Frankfurt-am-Main and working for the newspaper *Frankfurter Allgemeine* – says, "I estimated that it was in the region of Giessen that the bombers had a turning point where they would change course. The visibility at the altitude at which we were flying was so good that we could even see burning aircraft a great distance from us. We flew for about ten to fifteen minutes in a northerly direction and reached the main bomber stream. The heading on which they were flying was readily distinguished because some were burning on the ground.

"My radio-operator got a number of good fixes but each time I had to break off the action as other night-fighters were attacking the same aircraft. Then, at about 0052 hours, he got another contact on his screen. My operator, Unteroffizier Bruno Zakrzewski, nursed his newfound quarry on his set and called out, 'Target ahead . . . climb a bit . . . steady. Left . . . left . . . a little higher. Easy . . . one thousand metres . . . eight hundred metres . . . six hundred metres . . .' At four hundred metres I saw the Lancaster ahead. I brought the Messerschmitt below and to the port of the bomber until its port wing was ringed in the sights of my side guns and fired. I assumed that at least some of the crew were able to save themselves by parachute, for the bomber caught fire slowly. We logged the shoot-down about twenty-five to thirty kilometres north-west of Schweinfurt.

"Keeping a sharp look-out, we flew quite near to the searchlights and were able to see another bomber catch fire and dive to the ground. It had been caught in the beams. Later, we learned that it had been shot down by our squadron leader, Oberleutnant Tham.

"I then called my air-gunner, Obergefreite Fritz Sagner, and told him to change the ammunition drums on the oblique guns. Meanwhile, my radio-operator was able to lead me on to another bomber; but in his excitement my gunner took longer than usual to change the drums and I had to shadow the bomber, keeping one hundred and twenty metres beneath it while I followed all its movements. Without warning, it corkscrewed – although I was certain it had not seen us.

"At the moment I decided to attack from behind using the horizontal guns, my gunner reported that the oblique guns were now working. I tried again to land my shots between the two port engines, but the bomber suddenly swerved to port so that my fire landed in the port and star-board wings. Both wings burst into flames and the bomber dived sharply. This shooting-down was about 0104 hours, probably south-east of Schweinfurt.

"The fourth shooting-down followed at 0112 hours. I was again led on to the target by my radio-operator. We must have hit an important point in the fuselage, because the aircraft burst into flames and threatened to drop down upon us. I immediately threw my fighter into a steep dive.

It reached a critical speed and it was only with great difficulty that I managed to regain control. We lost at least a thousand metres before the machine answered to the controls again. The shooting-down took place south of Bamberg.

"I remember that after the last shooting-down, and especially after the steep dive, I was feeling very exhausted. I also had to look for a landing strip as we had already been two hours in the air. We picked up the radio-beacon of our base, took a northerly course, and landed at Erfurt at 0155 hours.

"When most of the crews were back and the night-fighters housed in the hangars, a long-range Mosquito intruder flew low over our base and raked the hangars with long bursts of fire. Ironically, my Messerschmitt – unscathed by its four combats – was among the machines hit. Its radiator cooling system and propeller were damaged."

Hauptmann Fritz Lau of IV/NjG 1 at Loan-Athies was as surprised as Seuss at being alerted that night. Lau, now working at Kiel Airport, was no newcomer to flying. He had been a civil pilot with the old Lufthansa before the war and had since gained much experience at night-fighting. Yet he, too, was proved wrong in his predictions when the order to scramble was given at 2300 hours.

The crews sprinted to their Me.110s, pulling their helmets on as they ran, while on the tarmac flight-mechanics were still clambering over the night-fighters and warming them up. Every other second there was a deafening roar as another engine came to life: and as some machines bumped over the grass as their pilots moved into take-off positions, others were run-up at full throttle to test their magnetos.

Lau, followed by his wireless-operator Unteroffizier Helmut Voellen, dropped into the cockpit of his Messerschmitt and clipped on his safety belt. His gunner, Obergefreite Egon Reinecke, took his position behind them.

Immediately, Lau thumbed down his switches – and cursed: the ground-crew had forgotten to fuel the fighter.

In a fever of impatience, he had to wait as the Messerschmitt was fuelled from a tanker while around him other fighters were gunned up and turned into the wind. Then the engines roared into a new pitch as the squadron streaked down the runway – all airborne now except for him. But a few minutes later he was able to take off after them, setting course for the east. It was almost 2354 hours.

"We had flown for about thirty minutes when I saw a plane going down on fire," Lau recalls. "When we burned, we flamed white. When the enemy burned, he burned dark red. I remember that during this night I saw only two white burn-ups.

"We had reached about five thousand five hundred metres when the radio-operator reported a contact on the radar. I flew towards it and recognised a four-engined bomber. The enemy pilot was weaving in a crocodile line. Perhaps he may have seen us, but more likely he was doing this to fly through the many burn-ups in the sky. I tried to get into an attack position. But each time I thought I had the bomber in my sights he moved out of them. At one moment I was a hundred and fifty metres away, the next two hundred metres. This went on for about two minutes. He weaved, I weaved. Gradually I came to the conclusion that I would lose him unless I did something fast. I decided that the next time I got into a reasonably close position I would attack.

"The moment came when the bomber, which was somewhat higher than us, went into a gradual right-hand turn and I turned with him. The distance between us was now about a hundred to a hundred and fifty metres. I pulled on the stick, lifted the Messerschmitt's nose and fired. Flames shot from the bomber and he went into a steep dive.

"I flew over him and saw three of the crew baling out. Before hitting the ground, the bomber broke into two parts – of which one, the larger, again broke on impact so that in the end three parts of it were burning below. The time was 0044 hours and, according to a radio-bearing fix we took, the spot must have been south-west of Bonn. The exact type of bomber we were not able to ascertain.

"After I saw the first shoot-down, red flaming masses were falling out of the sky almost every minute. There was first an explosion on the ground as the bomber hit, then bursts from the flames. A great row of these fires could be seen. They clearly marked out on the ground the course the bombers were flying."

Up to the time of the Nuremberg raid, Lau had chalked up about seven thousand flying hours – a third of them at night. And he was surprised that on this occasion there was little or no return fire from the bombers he saw – even though, as he explains, "In such a situation the fighter pilot is always in a more favourable position than the bomber. The bomber has a more or less fixed course to fly. And on the run-in to the target he must keep to his altitude in order to be at the right height to bomb. The fighter, by comparison, could change his course or height as he wished and could break off or attack at will. With us it was usual to fly just a bit lower than the bombers so that we could see them clearly against the starlit sky. As against that, the bomber crews had to look down into the darkness and could not spot us – or, if they did, only for a fleeting moment.

"Why the bomber crews did not fire on me I do not know. Perhaps they did not know for certain that I was there; or they may not have wanted to reveal their presence and so attract the attention of the fighters. But more probably, I do not think they saw us."

Chapter Thirteen

In and out of the bomber stream the fighters darted; and with each run they sprayed the bombers with high-speed cannon and machine-gun trace, leaving flame among the pack. There was no shortage of contacts, and the blips on the fighters' radar screens danced wildly. As one vanished, another appeared. Some of the fighters began to operate in pairs along the edge of the bomber box, hunting and picking off the stragglers.

What a night of triumph it was for the twin-engined Me.110s and Ju.88s. To them were falling most of Harris's heavies, and the cart-wheeling balls of fire dropping earthwards were tangible evidence of the deadliness of their interceptions. Bomber Command was being slaughtered. The big protective box formation in which the bombers had started out was being systematically smashed, and splinters from it burned and sputtered far below.

Again and again the night-fighters wheeled and pumped endless streams of shells into the huge, black vulnerable wings which housed the fuel tanks of the bombers – often not breaking away until they were close to colliding with their prey. Tonight they were taking a terrible revenge for the nights the bombers had eluded them with diversionary tactics and dummy feints. And as they continued to wreak havoc, many of the German night-fighter crews wondered at the suicidal dead-straight course on which their adversaries were routed.

It was this self-same thing that had been worrying Flight Sergeant Tom Fogaty, D.F.M., from the very beginning. Fogaty, now of Exmouth, had had grave misgivings as soon as the route had been made known at briefing: for he and his crew, whose average age was twenty-three, were old hands at large-scale bombing raids and were used to quite different tactics.

Just as bothered were his navigator, Flying Officer P. H. Paddon; bomb-aimer, Flying Officer J. Ferris; wireless-operator, Sergeant J. H. Lomas; mid-upper gunner, Pilot Officer Jock Simpson; rear-gunner, Sergeant E. A. Banham; and flight-engineer, Sergeant J. Dams. They were part of No. 115 Squadron, which had recently converted from Stirlings to Lancasters; and this was their second operation in a Lancaster. In previous weeks, in their Stirling, they had attacked such formidable targets as Berlin, Stuttgart, Augsburg, Frankfurt and the hell-spot Essen.

His earlier doubts about the route came back to Fogaty shortly after crossing the German border. About fifty combat sightings had already been logged by Flying Officer Paddon – most of them in the southern part of the Ruhr and on the fringes of the bomber stream – and Fogaty had himself never seen so many aircraft going down in the thirteen operations he had so far completed. It looked to him as though the Me.110s and Ju.88s had been waiting for them.

But with the Ruhr behind him, and the combats that had been raging constantly on all sides becoming less frequent, Fogaty breathed a little easier. The Lancaster was now about fifty miles north-west of Mannheim at an altitude of 22,000 feet. In another thirty minutes, he reckoned, they should be over Nuremberg – a calculation that was confirmed when the intercom clicked and Paddon told him that their E.T.A. at the target would be 0120 hours. This meant that, despite the high winds and the fact that they were in the last wave of the force, they would be on time.

His elation was short-lived. At that moment a burst of cannon fire struck the aircraft, just as rear-gunner Banham was shouting that they should corkscrew starboard.

Fogaty at once flung the Lancaster into a tight right-hand

Air Vice-Marshal D. C. T. Bennett, C.B.E., D.S.O.

A Halifax III

'Bomber' Harris (left) with his deputy, Sir Robert Saundby

Wing Commander Pat Daniels, Pathfinder
leader on the Nuremberg raid

The R.A.F.'s 'blockbusters': a 4000 lb. bomb ready for loading

Briefing prior to the Nuremberg raid

A Junkers Ju.88-S-1

Air Vice-Marshal R. A. Cochrane, C.B., C.B.E., A.F.C.

Oberst im Generalstab Johannes J. Janke,
photographed in 1960

Oberleutnant Helmuth
Schulte, Staffelkapitan of the
4th night-fighter echelon of
the 2nd Gruppe of NJG/5 who
flew Me.110s from Parchim.
Schulte shot down four
bombers during the
Nuremberg raid

A Messerschmitt Me.110 in flight

General Josef 'Beppo' Schmid (front), chief of the supreme command position (the 1st Fighter Corps), with his chief of the general staff, Colonel Heiner Wittmer

dive. Sergeant Dams, who had been keeping a close eye on the engine gauges, exclaimed as he saw the oil pressure beginning to fall on the starboard inner. It was clear that they had been hit in that engine which, without oil pressure, would quickly overheat.

Dams, having reported this and received Fogaty's instruction to feather the starboard inner, pulled the feathering toggle and watched anxiously as the engine coughed out a stream of blue-grey smoke before spinning slowly to a stop.

Fogaty had in the meantime learned that they had lost the night-fighter in their corkscrew manoeuvre and was bringing the Lancaster back on course, checking that no one had been hurt before trimming it to the heading on which it had been flying. There was an unhealthy smell of petrol and oil in the cockpit, and when he checked his instrument panel he saw that the altimeter needle was falling steadily. Trimming the aircraft again, he fixed his eyes on the altimeter. They were losing height at the rate of five hundred feet a minute: and the control column was sluggish and not responding as it should.

In ten minutes they had lost five thousand feet, and the altimeter needle was still slicing back. Each additional minute was costing them a precious five hundred feet in height. Fogaty realised that they were never going to reach Nuremberg. If they were to maintain any height at all they would have to jettison the bomb-load.

Flying Officer Ferris, the Canadian bomb-aimer, clicked down the bombing switches. If he *had* to jettison, he would release the bombs live in the hope that they might hit something or someone. He called on Fogaty to open the bomb-doors, confirmed that he had, and pressed the bomb tit. That would release the photo-flash and lessen the risk of an explosion on board, he considered. Then he slammed the jettison bar across to clear any hang-ups.

Fogaty knew that the bombs had gone when the control column kicked hard against his hands as the Lancaster bucked, freed from its load. He asked his navigator for a course to join the homeward track and began the turn. The Lancaster's rate of descent had been slowed to about two hundred feet a minute by jettisoning the bombs; but its air-speed was also reduced as soon as it began heading into the high winds that had just been behind it.

Fogaty swung them on to their new course and they were about thirty-five to forty miles west of the target, maintaining a height of 15,000 feet, when the ground guns found them. They guessed it to be predicted fire, for the heavy-calibre shells were bursting in neat groups around them, showering the night with a kaleidoscope of splintered ochre light. Shrapnel from the bursts rattled along the bomber's fuselage, and it pitched and rolled in the blasts created by exploding shells.

After what seemed an eternity, although it was in fact only a few minutes, they were clear of the barrage and Fogaty asked his flight-engineer to check on what damage had been done. Sergeant Dams made a quick inspection and reported nothing more serious than a few flak holes in the airframe.

The bomber continued on three engines. It was now on its own – a solitary target which could be easily picked up by ground radar.

Fogaty found that the controls were becoming increasingly difficult to handle, and he was sure that something somewhere had been severed – but he had no idea what. Then, when they were approximately forty-five to fifty miles south-west of Stuttgart, something gave in the controls, the control column felt light and limp in Fogaty's hands, and the bomber slipped into a shallow dive to starboard. Again the altimeter needle began to dip, and the entire aircraft started to shudder in an alarming manner.

It was clear that far greater damage had been done to the Lancaster than had at first been thought. The altimeter showed that they were now down to two thousand five hundred feet. They would never reach the enemy coast, let alone their base. There was only one solution . . . Fogaty called up his crew and told them to bale out.

Flying Officer Ferris, the bomb-aimer, was the first to go. From the rear-turret Sergeant Banham shouted that he was stuck. Simpson, the mid-upper gunner, scrambled from his turret to go to Banham's assistance and made his way along the fuselage as the Lancaster skidded and lurched on its ever-quickening downwards course. Reaching the rear-turret, he began to turn it manually so that Banham could escape and was rewarded with the thumbs-up sign from the rear-gunner, who then tumbled into space. Simpson slipped on his own parachute, informed Fogaty that the rear-gunner had safely baled out, and then made his own exit. Flying Officer Paddon and Sergeant Lomas followed him.

Only Fogaty and flight-engineer Dams were left. Fogaty glanced at the altimeter and saw that they were down to one thousand feet. If they were going to jump at all, it would have to be now. He unfastened his safety harness and motioned to Dams to hand him his parachute. Dams was waving his arms and pointing under the pilot's seat, indicating that his own parachute had become jammed under the seat by their earlier evasive action.

Fogaty's reaction was instantaneous. "Quick," he called, "take mine. There's no time to lose."

The flight-engineer hesitated, knowing that his pilot would be left with no means of escape. Fogaty shouted at him again to take the parachute and jump. Dams put Fogaty's parachute on and jumped clear at just under one thousand feet.

Alone in the doomed Lancaster, Fogaty considered his position. He knew beyond doubt that he now had no chance of getting out; and with his safety straps undone – even if he accomplished the seemingly impossible feat of a crash-landing – he would certainly be hurled from his seat on impact. It was bad enough to have to land a crippled aircraft on a well-lit home base with an engineer to operate the throttle levers while the gunner kept the tail down; but to make such an attempt single-handed in the middle of

Germany in pitch blackness would be seemingly impossible.

But with life there was hope – no matter how slender. And anyway, he asked himself, what alternative was there? If this was to be the end, at least he'd go out trying.

The sound of his own laboured breathing came to him over the intercom as he peered through the perspex and tried to find out what sort of terrain he was coming down over; but it was too dark for him to make anything out. Every muscle in his taut, tired body was now keyed to making a belly-landing, and he somehow managed to keep the Lancaster fairly straight as he lowered full flap.

At five hundred feet he switched on his landing lights and saw the ground rearing in front of him. Earth and sky seemed to merge as he struggled with the now almost-useless control column. He caught a glimpse of an orchard blurring beneath him and a stamp-sized patch which might have been a field.

Twenty feet from the ground, seeing what looked like a carpet of snow, he cut the engines, braced his wrists behind the control column and prayed. An overwhelming, jarring pain lanced through his forehead as an avalanche of roaring sound consumed the Lancaster, and he had a vague sensation of floating in a vacuum of utter darkness. And then – nothing.

Fogaty will never be sure of exactly what happened in those last minutes. "When I came to," he recalls, "I was lying in the snow some fifty yards from the aircraft. I vaguely remember seeing a small fire in one of the engines. There were several people who looked like farmers around me, and they took me to a farmhouse about a hundred yards away. None of them could speak English and I could not speak German.

"I was very confused. I had a huge bump on my forehead, a grazed leg and was minus one of my flying boots.

"After a short wait at the farmhouse, I was taken in a van to the police station of a nearby town. I have recently studied a detailed map of the area in which I came down, but I cannot recognise the name of the town. My navigator remembers climbing a signpost which said sixty-eight kilometres to Stuttgart, which he thought was north-east.

"I stayed, for what remained of the night, in a cell. The rest of the crew were brought in at intervals. The last to arrive was Jack Lomas, the wireless-operator. They were all surprised to see me – especially Johnny Dams, the engineer. He couldn't believe that I had managed to land the Lancaster alone.

"The interrogating officer in Frankfurt later told me that I was shouting 'Voici . . . voici . . .' when I was found. Presumably, I must have thought I had landed over the French border."

Fogaty's brilliance as a bomber pilot had already brought him the D.F.M., for which his citation in the *London Gazette* of 15th February 1944 read:

> This airman was the pilot of an aircraft which attacked targets in Brunswick one night in January 1944. Soon after leaving the target area the aircraft was intercepted by a fighter which attacked with much persistence. The bomber was hit in many places by the enemy's bullets. One engine was rendered useless, the front and mid-upper turrets were put out of action and the aircraft became filled with smoke.
>
> Nevertheless, Flight Sergeant Fogaty succeeded in evading the attacker. Although height was gradually lost on the homeward flight, Sergeant Fogaty reached base, where he effected a masterly landing. In very trying circumstances this airman displayed great skill and coolness and set a very inspiring example.

But though his commission came through while he was a prisoner-of-war, Fogaty received no official acknowledgment from the Air Ministry for his courage in handing his parachute to a crew member and then going on to perform the fantastic and incredible feat of landing a crippled four-engined bomber single-handed in darkness and in unknown territory.

Chapter Fourteen

Air Vice-Marshal Bennett's crack Pathfinder force, No. 8 Group, arrived over Fulda at approximately 0048 hours and swung on to a south-easterly heading for the bomb-run on Nuremberg. Behind them, and the leading main-force aircraft tailing them, lay the nearly-four-hundred-kilometres leg from Charleroi, now strewn with the flaming wreckage of some fifty bombers.

There was not a man in any of the bombers who did not sigh with relief – for it was hoped that the long-awaited change of course would throw off the night-fighters that had been harrying them ceaselessly since passing Aachen. But it was a forlorn hope. The fighters wheeled with them.

In the battle-opera-room of the 7th Jagddivision at Schleissheim, the ground controllers followed the turn on their plotting charts and marked the bombers as they swung out of grid square OB and down into grid square PB. And now there was no doubt whatsoever. Only one city lay directly in the path of the British force . . . Nuremberg.

The early-warning sirens of the city, which had been sounded as a precaution at 0035 hours, now wailed out to proclaim that an air-raid was imminent while ground transmitters blared to defence positions: "Enemy bomber formations leaving grid PB . . . approaching grid QB . . . target Nuremberg. More formations entering grid OB and lancing into grid PB."

Without delay, amid mounting tension, guns and searchlights of the Nuremberg defences were readied for the order which would belch a barrage of predicted fire into the sky above the city.

In the blacked-out noses of Pathfinder Lancasters, bomb-aimers had already spread out in front of them their two-feet-long large-scale target maps, lithographed in purple, grey and white and showing the built-up areas and main features of the city. Rings drawn on the maps rippled out from the centre at a scaled-down distance of one mile from each other for the pinpointing of specific sections.

Wing Commander Pat Daniels, the first in the Pathfinder force to orbit the target, saw that the city was covered by seven-tenths cloud ... which meant that the attack would have to be delivered – as had been anticipated at briefing – by means of Wanganui, the sky-marking technique that was the least accurate of Bomber Command's target-marking methods. Heavy broken cloud rolled under his Lancaster, forming vast canyons through which the moonlight glowed; and columns of light from the searchlights now groped along this cloud base as they sought the openings leading to the cold bright stars. Piercing the billowing carpet of cloud, shells from the ground guns were bursting in brilliant flashes of red-orange fury among the cloud-peaks and leaving neat interwoven pockmarks in the clear sky above.

At 0105 hours the first of the Pathfinder Wanganui flares fell in vivid cascades of dazzling red, floating above the cloud layers and swinging gently to and fro under their parachutes. Interspersed among them were clusters of emerald-green stars. They were followed by showers of red indicators, which fell over the city like fiery Christmas trees. Then came more red flares, blazing and spluttering and giving to those below whose duty it was to watch the impression that the very clouds were afire.

At 0106 hours, plumb in the middle of this deadly pyro-technic exhibition, there were released still more red flares, this time shooting out clusters of yellow stars from their centres. And at 0107 hours the six 'visual' Pathfinder Lancasters swept in and released ground markers through the centre of the Wanganui flares, followed a minute later by a strong formation of blind-sky-marker Lancasters which dropped its candelabras among the still-twinkling illuminators of the leaders. Behind them came more visual markers, who unloaded further clusters of target indicators, and at 0109 hours both sky and ground were exposed to yet more flares as the Pathfinder force's supporters droned over the city.

The timing of the Pathfinders had been good. Wing Commander Daniels, banking his aircraft to begin a second orbit of the city, saw that some of the main-force bombers which had arrived earlier than they should have were levelling out for their bomb-runs.

At 0110 hours the first wave of the main-force Lancasters and Halifaxes fanned over Nuremberg on a broad front. But the city was to suffer less than the full fury of the concentrated saturation raid planned – and not only because of the determination with which the German night-fighter squadrons had decimated the bomber force on the long, straight run from Charleroi to Fulda. Some of the bombers were operating on misjudged wind-speeds, and their bombs overshot the city. Others, through similar navigational errors, combats with fighters and/or poor visibility, also completely missed the city with their bombs.

The great mass of Harris's heavies were now over or only a few miles from Nuremberg: but so, too, were the fighters – like tenacious terriers, still trying to harry and savage them. The havoc caused by the fighters, coupled with the high winds, bedevilled the opening stages of the attack. Bombers were coming in from all directions, some of their crews releasing their bombs haphazardly in their eagerness to get away as quickly as possible.

To the crews of bombers on the lower height-band, the risk of a collision or of being struck by a stray 4000-pounder from aircraft above was now more frightening than the searchlights and the flak. And as if to exploit this new fear scarecrow rockets suddenly started to shoot up from the ground to burst among the heavy-calibre anti-aircraft shells with the impression of bomb-loads exploding.

Adding to the confusion, night-fighter flares began to drift from above and intermingle with the British target illuminators. As a further reminder to bomber crews that the Me.110s and Ju.88s were still around, the familiar bright tracer shells of the night-fighters flashed spasmodically across the sky.

To the men in the bombers, Nuremberg now had all the appearances of a city under a mass air-attack. Through gaps in the cloud, extensive areas of fire could be observed; and thousands of tiny points of dark red light flickered below as incendiaries burned.

More blind-illuminator-marker aircraft, loaded with white parachute flares and red target indicators, made their marking run: but the brilliance of the flares was swiftly dimmed by the massive banks of cloud rolling over the city. In their first blinding galaxy of light the sky seemed to be full of four-pound sticks of incendiaries hurtling and twisting from the bomb-bays of the heavies.

Wing Commander Daniels swept his Lancaster across the city for its third circuit of the target, and he noted with anxiety that the bombing was becoming increasingly erratic. Twenty miles north of the city there had been little cloud, but now whirling mists and curling peaks of dense vapour were obscuring the markers and spoiling the accuracy of the bomb-aimers. Daniels, having spent nearly twenty-five minutes over Nuremberg, swung the Lancaster in a broad arc and headed for home. There was nothing more to be done, and he would need every drop of fuel for the long and hazardous return flight.

Daniels' flight-commander, Squadron Leader Keith Creswell, also banked his Lancaster on to the homeward course. He, too, had a strong feeling that the attack was not as successful as it might have been. His first quick circuit of the city as the leader of the primary visual markers over the target had made it plain to him that because of the amount of cloud the marking would have to be done by Wanganui. Because of this, as his squadron's records show, he released his markers and then bombed on radar. As he had suspected, the sixty-mile-an-hour winds encountered over the target – though not as strong as those battled against earlier – were powerful enough to disperse many of the sky-markers. Consequently, the bombing was poorly concentrated and very spasmodic.

By now, the second wave of Lancasters and Halifaxes had converged over the city, their black shapes clearly outlined by the moonlight. The unmistakable vapour trails they had left behind them were an open invitation to the night-fighters, so they hurriedly unloaded their bombs and then dropped in fast dives to clear the target area.

The combination of cloud and moonlight minimised for the bomber crews the harsh vulgarity of the fires taking hold in the streets and squares below them. But nothing – not the fighters, the guns, the searchlights or the terrifying scarecrow shells – could now prevent the bombers that had got through from dropping their devastating cargo.

Bomb-aimers, their eyes glued to the cross-hilts of their glowing graticle sights, rapped out the bombing drill fast and clear; and the great aircraft they were in bucked and reared as their swollen bellies were relieved. But even as the harbingers of death sped towards the city, death was in the air. One plane disintegrated on its bomb-run and showered a Halifax close by with fiery fragments. Another slid into a slow glide as fire licked its wing. Not far away a violent explosion seemed to rend the sky as two bombers collided over the target area.

Halifax L-Love of No. 158 Squadron, from Lisset, was about to start its bomb-run when a fighter – which the crew took to be an Me.110 – opened fire. Sergeant Reginald Cripps, in the rear-turret, saw the trace and called for a corkscrew to port, whereupon Flight Sergeant Stan Windmill, the pilot, rolled the bomber into a left-hand dive. By the time they came out of it there was no sign of the fighter, but about one hundred yards to their port was another Halifax with its starboard outer-engine ablaze. It was L-Love's second lucky brush with a fighter. Earlier in the flight, Cripps had been puzzled by the antics of a twin-engined fighter flying astern of them with its navigation lights on. It had kept well out of range of the Halifax's Brownings, firing periodic bursts of cannon fire at them without success. When a bomber below and to their starboard had opened up on it with a long burst of tracer, it had sheered off and disappeared. Would they be so fortunate a third time? Cripps wondered as L-Love levelled off for the bomb-run and dropped its complement of bombs through seven-tenths cloud.

The crew of Lancaster G-George of No. 460 R.A.A.F. Squadron had not been fooling themselves that the run-in on Nuremberg would be easy. But they were comforted by the knowledge that their aircraft had had the phenomenal luck to come through eighty-six missions so far, trusting that Nuremberg would be the eighty-seventh.

Remembering the operation, G-George's flight-engineer, Sergeant Holder, says, "It was a story of the perfect air ambush and Germany's greatest single defensive success in the grim cat-and-mouse game that was played out for nearly six years between the bombers and the fighters.

"The ground controllers had to guess where we were making for, and they guessed correctly. We were heading for the Stuttgart 'gap' – a small opening in the great flak belt. When we reached it there were hundreds of German fighters waiting in the brilliant moonlight to shoot down our heavily-laden bombers – and they downed us by the score. Fifty miles from the target all hell was let loose. There were enemy fighters everywhere. We were sitting ducks, with no cloud cover to shield us. We counted twelve of our aircraft going down in almost as many minutes, all of them in flames. Sometimes we could see two or three night-fighters peeling away from one of our crippled bombers.

"Usually when we saw an aircraft going down or blowing up we reported it to the navigator, who made a brief note of the time and position; but on this raid it would have been a full-time job for him, so he told us to forget it.

"During the heat of the battle we began to wonder when our turn would come. All the time, tracer fire was criss-crossing the sky. Bombers were taking violent evasive action, so one didn't really know what was actually happening. But if a red glow appeared, we knew it was one of ours.

"Over the target it was chaotic. Bombers were sweeping in from all directions, unloading their bombs and getting out as fast as they could. It was obvious that the stream was disorganised before it ever reached Nuremberg. The run-in was nerve-racking as we had to watch for other bombers suddenly swerving across our track. But with luck, or perhaps skill on our bomb-aimer's part, we made a perfect run over the target. The ack-ack was fairly intense, but I thought they were firing at random. Yet even over the city the fighters were mixing it with us.

"After we dropped our bombs, our pilot shouted over the intercom for us to get the hell out of it and rammed the throttles through the gate. He screamed into a dive and the Lancaster shuddered with the speed of it. This worried me as I had to watch our fuel consumption, and such action burned it up.

"The bomber gunners put up a brave show against terrific odds. At one period near the target we saw one Lancaster on fire from nose to tail, yet the gunners were still firing until it eventually blew up.

"I was amazed that there were not more collisions over the target. One bomber missed our tail by inches, and our rear-gunner coolly remarked that if he had thrust out his hand he could have shaken hands with its pilot. Before this hellish action we had bombed many big German cities – such as Berlin, Essen, Frankfurt and Stuttgart – but this was our first real experience of encountering the full fury of the enemy's fighter force . . . and it was terrifying."

Flying Officer Bill Clegg, bomb-aimer of No. 44 Squadron's Y-Yorker, had just stretched himself along his bombing mat when he realised that it was going to be tricky to bomb – for above, below and on each side of his Lancaster other bombers were making the run, their bomb-bays open. Around him, the glaring flashes of their camera flares were proof that they were ignoring their bombing heights. He could see some of the red target indicators burning on the ground, but before he could level them in his sights other aircraft recklessly swung on to them, seemingly oblivious to the collision risks they were taking.

Clegg was an experienced bomb-aimer who had been through too much to let his bombs go at random. The 'panic' crews could drop theirs heedlessly and get the hell out of it. He didn't really blame them. But there would be other nights – and if panic got him tonight, it might get him again in the future. It just wouldn't be worth it.

He called for another orbit of the city and heard someone groan over the intercom, but Wing Commander Thompson hauled the Lancaster into a shallow turn and cautiously began the circuit. As the second run began, Clegg noticed that the cloud veiling the city was now gradually thinning. And then he saw a dying target indicator winking teasingly at him from below. It was just what he needed. He thumbed forward the drift handle of his Mark 14 bombsight, slapped down his selector switches and fused his bombs.

Thompson had just seen the light appear on his panel to confirm that the bomb-doors had opened when out of the night another bomber side-slipped in front of Y-Yorker. The Wing Commander jabbed on right rudder, dropped the nose of the Lancaster and cursed the black shape that now flashed past above them. It appeared to him that the bomber crews now had only one thing in mind – to get quickly away from Nuremberg regardless.

For the third time Y-Yorker made its bomb-run, and this time the approach was clear. But although the crew breathed heavily in relief as the bomb-load left them, they could not now thrust on full throttle and, like the other bombers, dive away from the target. They still had a job to do – the perilous one of photographing and assessing the damage below, for which it was necessary for Thompson to take the Lancaster down to 10,000 feet and begin a straight run across the city with cameras whirring.

It was quieter now, by comparison. The bulk of the bombers had gone and the flak was lighter, but the mission was nonetheless dangerous. If nothing else, there were still some of their own aircraft to contend with. As when Flight Lieutenant Burrows, the flight-engineer, glanced out over Y-Yorker's starboard wing and saw something that made his eyes glaze with horror. A Lancaster was coming straight at them.

"Dive . . . dive!" he screamed.

Thompson's reaction was amazingly fast for a man who had been flying for over four hours, mostly through an inferno. He thrust the control column forward and threw the Lancaster into a sickening diving turn . . . Black wings and glowing exhausts flashed overhead in the airspace they had left a moment before.

Says Burrows, 'How we missed each other is still something we discuss even now when we meet."

But miss they did; and Y-Yorker – one of the last of the Lancasters to leave Nuremberg – swung on course for England with its mission accomplished.

Chapter Fifteen

At the height of the attack on Nuremberg one particularly large explosion was observed in the target area. "We were on our run-up when we saw it," relates Flight Sergeant C. P. Steedman of Parry Town, Ontario, Canada, a Lancaster bomb-aimer on his twenty-sixth operational flight. "At the time, the whole area was covered by cloud – and the target was further obscured by the condensation trails left by our bombers, which criss-crossed over the target and caused a layer of haze through which we had to fly – but the light of this explosion flashed up in a bright orange glow. It lasted for some seconds." And it seemed to indicate that something of strategic importance had been well and truly hit.

But many bomber crews, even over the target, were still concerned with night-fighter combats. Flight Sergeant E. Oberhardt of Maryborough, Queensland, Australia, a Lancaster rear-gunner, reported, "We were going in to bomb when we saw a Junkers 88 about three hundred and fifty yards away. I warned my skipper and gave the fighter a burst as it came in from the port side. Then it went over to starboard. I had my guns trained on it as it snooped below. I saw tracer going through its fuselage, and it soon made off. Other combats were going on near us at the same time.

"A shell from the Junkers went through our starboard wing, near the starboard inner-engine, and left a very large hole. A few minutes later, the engine began to get troublesome and we had to feather it. In the end, it stopped altogether. We made our way home on three engines."

Another Australian, Lancaster pilot Flight Sergeant

N. D. L. Lloyd of Winton, Northern Queensland, recalls, "During our run-up, I was told that a fighter had seen us. It kept away until we had dropped our bombs and then came for us. It was an FW.190. My gunners were ready for it, and after a sharp exchange of fire it made off. A few minutes later, another fighter took up the challenge. It was a better stayer than the first one, and we didn't shake it off until it had followed us for about ten minutes."

Also remembering the night-fighter activity, Flight Lieutenant T. R. Donaldson of Brighton, Victoria, Australia, a Lancaster pilot, says, "There were fighters all the way, and they were making the most of the bright moon. I watched tracer flashing across the sky as bomber after bomber fought its way to the target. The Germans were doing their damnedest to beat us off. Searchlights . . . flak . . . and fighters . . ."

But Flight Lieutenant C. G. Broughan, a Halifax pilot from Sydney, Australia, clearly felt that the fighters had done their worst before the target was reached when he reported, 'There was cloud over the city, but it was broken. Through the gaps we saw fires getting a firm hold. The Pathfinders had marked out the area with sky and ground markers; and though there had been scores of fighters along the route, there was not enough of them over the target to interfere seriously with the bombing."

Sergeant Rowlinson, whose Lancaster H-Harry had earlier been attacked by a fighter, was relieved to see Nuremberg. When his plane arrived over the city shortly after 0109 hours the target was well marked with green and red illuminators, around which large fires were burning.

Flight Lieutenant Startin, H-Harry's pilot, was not saying much. He held the wheel tightly and his eyes darted everywhere, looking for trouble but hoping not to find it. His aircraft seemed enormous and he felt as though it was the only one in the sky. Every gun down below must surely be vectored on him, and their flashes looked vicious, sharp and deadly. He wouldn't have believed that to the Germans his Lancaster was one of the many hundreds of spots on their cathode-ray tubes, for he was certain that he was their sole target.

Flight Sergeant Ben Lawrence, the twenty-two-year-old bomb-aimer, brought H-Harry on to the bomb-run at a height of 19,000 feet and called on Startin to open the bomb-doors. More Pathfinder flares were being dropped, and within seconds they burst and cascaded over the ground – a mass of green balls that shone brightly, like fairy lights.

"There it is, skipper – straight ahead. Keep her steady," Lawrence called, watching the indicators as they crawled up his sword-sight. "Steady – right; right; hold it – ste–ady." Eight seconds to go.

On all sides, other bomb-aimers were going through the same drill as the run-in began through a curtain of steel splinters. Heavy anti-aircraft shells were coming up all around them, leaving black puffs which floated past at an alarming speed. Searchlights danced crazily in front of them, trying to find a victim. And from above came night-fighter flares, followed by Me.110s and Ju.88s which darted in and out like sombre vultures as they delivered their attack.

The petrified sky seemed to be full of tracer bullets – some curving up, some curving down, and others hose-piping horizontally – as here and there a bomber's rear-gunner let loose with his Brownings.

With five seconds to go, Lawrence called for a touch more right rudder.

Still the flares were going down, still the tracer was coming up, and still combats were taking place left, right and centre. There were bombers exploding after direct hits and falling from the sky, leaving a wide trail of black smoke as they disintegrated far below. Flak was everywhere. And although many of the leading bombers had been shot down, wave after wave of those behind droned over the city's boundaries and headed for the city centre.

H-Harry continued flying dead level, but the short time they had been on the bomb-run seemed like an eternity to the crew. They watched great sticks of incendiaries showering over the target-indicator markers, looking hardly bigger than matchsticks from their height.

With only three seconds to go, Lawrence called, "Steady – hold it . . ." And then, "Bombs gone." There was relief in his voice.

Free of its load, the bomber leapt forward; and Startin, after pulling the jettison toggle to release any bombs that might still be on the racks, kept on a dead-straight course while the Lancaster's camera photographed their aiming point.

Lawrence, peering from the aircraft's nose, saw his bombs splash across the city, the incendiaries bursting in tiny points of white light which turned to a dark red as the fires took hold.

Startin wheeled the bomber in a diving turn on to their outward course, warning his gunners to keep a sharp lookout since more fighter flares were falling from above.

Incendiaries from other bombers were still slapping in great sticks across the target-markers while the heavier 'cookies' exploded one after another with slow red glows; and photo-flashes could be seen at all heights among the flak and tracer as each bomber took pictures of its aiming point – the whole turning the night sky into a blazoning of varicoloured exploding light . . . and a living nightmare to those flying in it.

Fires started by the spearhead bombers had now taken a hold, and against their vivid flames could be seen the lower-height-band squadrons flying steadily on over the battered city.

Rowlinson continued his close watch on Fishpond – which had saved them more than once that night – and soon saw the now-familiar blip of a fighter as it moved on to his screen from their port quarter. He quickly alerted the gunners.

Hopkinson, in the rear-turret, spotted the fighter almost immediately; and as Startin slid the Lancaster into a dive, both gunners opened up on the fighter. In the chaos around them they could not tell whether or not they had hit it, but the fighter didn't return to the attack. Nevertheless, the incident encouraged them to get out while they could and, with bombers still going down around them, Startin weaved and corkscrewed H-Harry until they were well clear of the target.

Lancaster E-Easy of No. 625 Squadron, No. 1 Group, approached Nuremberg with its rear-turret out of action. A mechanical fault had developed and, although the turret could still be turned, its guns would not fire. By the time the crew had discovered this it was too late to go back. But luck was with them. Despite the many combats that raged around them, they reached Nuremberg without being attacked.

Their flight-engineer, Flight Lieutenant N. R. Truman D.F.C., says, "We began our bombing-run at twenty thousand feet and were aghast to see masses of vapour trails from the bombers ahead of us which plainly showed our track to the fighters. We became increasingly conscious of very considerable fighter activity. Everywhere one looked there were unmistakable signs of air-to-air firing. With our rear-turret useless, we decided to get in and out fast. Once we had dropped our bombs, we increased power and began to gradually shed height to give us greater speed. It was contrary to our briefing orders but we were determined to get away from those tell-tale vapour trails. And it was a tactic that paid off, for E-Easy again had the phenomenal luck of reaching the coast unscathed."

Lack of sleep was beginning to tell on the crew of Pathfinder D-Don of No. 156 Squadron, all of whom had returned from leave that day. In the rear-turret, Flight Sergeant 'Tubby' Holley could hardly keep his eyes open.

He'd been at the railway station at 0530 hours to catch a train to his base: but if he'd known then that he would be going straight out on an 'op' ... Damn! Tiredness washed over him in waves.

D-Don, a primary-blind-marker Lancaster, was one of the first to take off for Nuremberg. On its flight south of the Ruhr its crew observed several combats, and Holley reported four or five bombers going down in almost as many minutes. Flight Lieutenant Bagg, who was on his second tour of operations, then picked up his first blip on Fishpond. It was about one mile to port of them.

Holley peered into the darkness but could see nothing. A moment later, Bagg reported that there was another fighter two miles to starboard; but again Holley was unable to get a visual on it. The blips then vanished from the screen and the gunners were informed that the fighters had gone. It was just as well – for quite apart from the terrible lethargy he felt, Holley had guns that were not working and he would therefore have been unable to do anything even if they were attacked.

Fighting off a fresh spasm of weariness, he was fervently hoping that they would soon reach Nuremberg when Bagg's voice jerked him from his reverie with a report that he had picked up more fighters on his screen. Again Holley failed to see them, and again they failed to materialise.

Then came the words for which he had been anxiously waiting. D-Don's navigator, Flying Officer Jones, was announcing the course for the run-in to the target. It was the cue for bomb-aimer Flying Officer Blackadder to lift the bombing-tit from its socket as he watched the outskirts of Nuremberg appear on his H2S radar bombing screen.

Recalling the bomb-run, Holley says, "I felt tired and had a job to keep my eyes open. The flak was moderate. But even the thought of a fighter on our tail was not worrying me all that much I was so tired. Somehow or other I just about managed to keep the turret swinging, looking out now and then at the searchlights. 'Blackie' released our target indicators, the 'cookie' and other bombs with the aid of H2S. Then came the worst part as we flew straight and level over the target with our camera whirring. Now and then the Lancaster pitched and rocked from the concussion of bursting anti-aircraft shells. Next minute we were turning on to our course for the homeward journey.

"Before long, and in spite of all my efforts to stay awake, I felt my eyes closing. I don't suppose they were shut for more than a few seconds, for as my head dropped forward on to my chest I woke up and stared out of the turret, searching for fighters. And so it went on. As I came out of a doze I would stare into the darkness, then my head would go down and I'd drop off."

Hauptmann Lau, after he had shot down his Halifax, swung the Me.110 on to an easterly course. The failure of the ground-crews at Loan-Athies to refuel his fighter had seriously delayed him. About thirty Me.110s had taken off from the aerodrome – and his, he cursed, had to be the only one that had not been fuelled in readiness for a raid. Still, he had downed one bomber: and with a bit of luck he would catch up with the rest of his squadron.

Guided by air-to-air combats and the wreckage of burning bombers below, Lau neared Nuremberg shortly after 0100 hours, seeing the fires started by the bombs while still some distance from the city. "As we came nearer, I could see more and more bombs as they rained down," he remembers. "But when I reached the target, the bombing seemed to have stopped. At about seven thousand metres I flew over the burning town in the hope that in the bright light we might be able to detect the direction in which the bombers were making their getaway. But we did not sight any more, probably because I was so late."

Lau was nevertheless hopeful of getting into the action again on orders from his ground control. But here a new problem arose. Every bomber had its bundles of 'window' – of which it was reckoned that a dozen aircraft dropping the metal strips would appear on German radar screens like an erratic force of about nine hundred planes. And now, as the bombers turned for home, masses of 'window' were being released every half-minute or so. The new Lichtenstein SN2 sets with which the night-fighters had been equipped could penetrate its fuzz when the fighters were within range of the bombers; but the ground stations couldn't cope with it at all. It jammed their radar and seriously hampered their efforts to assess the homeward course of the enemy force.

Because of this, Lau received no new instructions from his ground control and therefore decided to climb. With more height, he hoped that he might spot the bombers silhouetted against the reflection of the flames rising from Nuremberg. And there was always a chance that while he was orbiting the city the outward course of the bombers might be flashed to him from the ground.

His orbit showed that the last of the invaders had gone. There was still some flak; but the searchlights, apart from a few to the east, had ceased to operate.

He made another sweep of the city but there were not even stragglers to be found, so he decided to continue on a westerly course. And as he flew on, his radar operator, Unteroffizier Helmut Voeller, sought to pick up the rearguard of the bomber force on his set. Perhaps luck would be with them and they would catch a random trace.

"Luck was not with us," Lau recalls. "Added to this, it was clear that the bombers, after unloading their bombs, were breaking out of their formation – each pilot taking his own course for England. In those circumstances, they could vary their headings and altitudes at will and this way better avoid us night-fighters.

"I reckoned there was no point in searching any longer, so I decided to land at Langediebach. At the base there was great activity on the runways as about seventy or eighty fighters had landed there. Because we had started late and were in no danger of running out of fuel, we let our comrades go down ahead of us and circled the field. We landed at 0225 hours and flew back to our own base at Loan-Athies later that morning."

The 2nd Gruppe of NJG 5 rose from the runways at Parchim in half-minute intervals from 2339 hours onwards with orders to cut off the bombers just south of the Rhine should they swing to the east, as was anticipated. By this time the ground controllers had well established the attack situation; and as the bomber force made its turn, the Me.110s were waiting for them near Stuttgart at an altitude of 6000 metres.

Oberleutnant Helmuth Schulte, Staffelkapitan of the 4th Echelon from Parchim, soon sighted his first Lancaster and brought his fighter slightly below and to the side of it. At a range of about fifty metres he fired with his oblique guns, but they jammed after a few rounds. Short though the burst had been, however, it was effective. The Lancaster's starboard inner engine blossomed into flame, and the bomber dropped into a diving turn with the Messerschmitt following closely in the bright moonlight.

Schulte positioned his fighter for another attack, but the crippled bomber had lost so much speed that he overshot it. He then came round for another attempt and this time thumbed a long stream of cannon shells into the already stricken plane, which rolled into a glide and exploded in clusters of red, green and white flame. This indicated that he had downed a Pathfinder, and he knew then that he must be in contact with the spearhead of the raiding force. He therefore climbed back to the height at which he had intercepted the Lancaster, recording that it had made impact at 0048 hours near Neckartzenlingen.

Shortly after this, his radar operator, Unteroffizier Sandvoss, reported that he had good contacts on his screen and vectored the Messerschmitt on to one of them. It turned out to be a Halifax. The Messerschmitt swept in on it and Schulte blasted it, again using his now-operable oblique guns. Coming out of the attack, he observed the bomber exploding near Woelferbuett. The time was 0113 hours.

Suspecting that his side-guns were going to jam again, Schulte called his mechanic and tail-gunner, Unteroffizier Fischer, who checked and confirmed that the firing pins were unserviceable. They were about to be replaced when another blip appeared on the radar screen. The fighter stalked it until Schulte was able to visually make out the dark outline of a Lancaster which, having manoeuvred the Messerschmitt into position, he raked with a long burst of cannon fire from his flank guns. As the bomber keeled over and exploded on the ground near Bischwind-bei-Bamberg, he checked the time and found that precisely thirteen minutes had elapsed between his second and third kill. And ahead of him he could now see the flames of Nuremberg.

Schulte flew over the city and immediately caught a glimpse of a twin-engined aircraft, but not clearly enough to tell whether it was a fellow night-fighter or a marauding Mosquito of the R.A.F.'s Night Striking Force. Before he could decide what to do about it, his attention was caught by the four glowing exhausts of what was unmistakably a British bomber. There was no hesitation this time. He at once skidded his fighter crabwise until he had the enemy in the sights of his flank armament, and then he fired. To his satisfaction, flames fanned from the bomber as it sucked in his cannon burst before breaking up into jagged fiery fragments just south of the city's boundaries. The time was 0130 hours; and Schulte, with four rapid shoot-downs to his credit, was eager to find another victim.

It didn't take long. The sickle moon, which had confounded the bombers, shone brightly in front of the Messerschmitt and highlighted the outline of another raider.

Schulte climbed slowly towards the port of the bomber and then whipped his fighter into a fast right-hand turn, at the same time stabbing his firing button. But nothing happened. He had forgotten to reload. His lapse, he thought angrily, was going to cost him the prey; but when he peered anxiously out, the raider was still there, flying on a fairly level course. Thankful for the second chance, he swept in again from the port quarter. As he fired his nose guns, however, the bomber plummeted into a steep corkscrew and he saw his shells pass harmlessly over it. Its gunners had obviously seen him, but not soon enough for them to fire.

Schulte searched for the bomber, but without success. It was the one that got away – from him, at least. But he couldn't complain: four kills and a near miss. Not bad, even if it had been exhausting.

As he says, looking back on the operation, "We were all getting very tired by this time; and because the raid had put so much strain on our nerves we decided that it would be best to get back to base. We landed at Mainz-Finthen at 0235 hours and when we checked found that we had fired fifty-six shells from the side cannon.

"When I consider the events of this night it seems to me that the first bombers were forced to go far to the south, while those behind them turned between Koblenz and Mainz-Frankfurt on an easterly heading. During our flight over Nuremberg, most of the attackers made their bombing-runs from north to south."

Chapter Sixteen

The first homeward flights began at about 0120 hours, with most of the bombers taking a westerly course before swinging on to a north-west heading. But there was little order in the manner of their going. As soon as they had dropped their bombs, the Lancasters and Halifaxes sped from Nuremberg in what became wide, loose gaggles – thus robbing themselves of the protection of a concentrated force. For once they were clear of the city, the German ground radar stations had less difficulty in piercing their widespread 'window'. German radar quickly traced those that flew over the line Frankfurt-Stuttgart and others that crossed the Brussels-Rheims sector; while many that had left the stream early were vectored as they passed over Cologne and Kassel.

The coast was a long way off, and the bombers that had fought their way to Nuremberg now had to fight their way back. And it wasn't only the enemy that they had to contend with. The high winds that had sent many of them hurtling past Nuremberg were now in front of them, and the bombers had to strain against them.

There was also something else for the crews to worry about – something that had troubled Air Marshal Saundby throughout the morning conference at Bomber Command Headquarters . . . the risk of them being caught in broad daylight while still over enemy territory. But there was no question of flying at top speed. Fuel consumption had to be carefully watched, and reluctant hands were forced to ease back on throttle levers.

The cold front the bombers were now flying through

presented yet another hazard – the danger of icing; and crews again cursed the Met men who had so completely misled them. Over the target had been moonlight instead of heavy cloud, and in place of the clear skies and lessening winds predicted for this stage of the operation there were cumulo-nimbus ice clouds. On a night when everything had gone wrong because of the weather, it was the weather that again had to be fought as well as the German night-fighters.

Remembering with bitterness the shambles of the route into Nuremberg, many pilots ignored the flight-plan back and charted their own courses home. And, inevitably, there was no semblance of concentration. The stream was spread high and wide. Uppermost in all minds was the need to get to the coast as speedily as possible. But bases were some four-hours' flying time away, and navigators were recording wind-speeds ranging from seventy to eighty miles an hour against them. It was a dismal prospect – particularly for pilots who, on checking their fuel consumption, knew that they would never make it because of the extra petrol used in evading fighters.

So the battle-worn Lancasters and Halifaxes faltered on, only to encounter massive cloud banks that had the appearance of snowy mountain peaks. Some pilots, because of the threat of icing, started to climb frantically above them; but many, rather than squander their precious fuel in climbing, decided to fly straight through and risk being holed by the high-velocity ice-bullets the clouds were capable of flinging at them.

Fear of the weather became every bit as great as fear of fighters as a raging storm now hammered the bombers – many of which were crippled and had dead and wounded men aboard. There seemed to be no end to the tumbling columns of ice clouds, and there was certainly no sign of the storm abating.

For many crews the faint qualms they'd had about ever returning were fast becoming serious doubts. They weren't fooling themselves that the worst was behind them. With fuel at a dangerously low level, ahead of them was the ordeal of getting through more enemy flak and fresh squadrons of night-fighters, after which would come the hurdle of the coastal defences. It was enough to occupy their thoughts without conjectures about whether they would be able to land when they reached their bases in England . . . *if* they reached England.

Their immediate task was to get clear of enemy territory.

Among the night-fighter pilots to go into action against the returning bombers as they swept out of Germany and into France was Hauptmann Ernst Modrow of the 1st Nachtjagdgeschwader, stationed at Venlo, north-east of Düsseldorf.

He had taken off earlier that night with orders to intercept in-flying Mosquitos and had spent two hours patrolling the Scheldt estuary and the Zuider Zee without seeing a single trace of the enemy.

His aircraft was a supercharged Heinkel 219 – the only German plane considered capable of combating the Mosquito. For it had long been proven that the Mosquito completely outmatched both the Me.110 and the Ju.88. Yet, oddly enough, the remarkable Mosquito had been turned down in the early days of the war by Air Ministry experts who argued that the aircraft – entirely made of wood – was unsuitable for night flying. It was, however, eventually recognised as one of the great assets of the R.A.F., and its roles were numerous. When used as a bomber, it could carry with ease a 4000 lb bomb to a target as far away as Berlin: and it needed only a two-man crew as compared with the seven-man crew required for a Lancaster or Halifax. In fact, many claimed that in its role as a bomber it was worth seven Lancasters. Moreover, being faster than the German night-fighters, its casualty rate was about one-tenth that of the Lancaster. Its top speed was nearly four hundred miles per hour, and it carried a formidable armament of four twenty-millimetre guns when used as a fighter. A not inconsiderable adversary. Hence Modrow and his supercharged Heinkel 219.

After his fruitless search, he landed at Venlo airfield at 0100 hours to be told that the whole of his group had gone into action against strong bomber formations approaching southern Germany. As it was too late for him to join them, he was assigned to intercepting the bombers on their homeward flight.

An hour and a half later, he was scrambled and put under the direction of the ground controller at Arnheim; but he soon found that his orders were being jammed by the bombers. He therefore relied on the heavy flak being fired at them to guide him to the outward course they were flying.

It was not long before his radar operator traced an enemy plane on his screen; and Modrow, who had never before operated with the SN2 close-range radar, was greatly impressed when the contact it had picked up turned out to be a Lancaster weaving and corkscrewing in shallow dives through the flak. Its tactics made it difficult for the fighter to stalk, but Modrow managed to follow it and twist and dive with it.

Clearly unaware that there was a fighter following him, the Lancaster pilot made a sudden weave that brought his aircraft right into the waiting sights of the Heinkel. Modrow fired his six wing and nose cannon and heard the shells slap into the bomber's starboard wing, throwing out chunks of metal from the inner engine. The Lancaster's wing exploded and Modrow was momentarily blinded by the glare – almost disastrously, for as he banked into a steep starboard turn he came into the sights of the British reargunner. A hail of scissor-fire was raked into the Heinkel's belly, but most of it was deflected by the plane's strong undercarriage.

Modrow watched as the Lancaster fell awkwardly, to crash in the region of Abbeville at approximately 0413 hours; and he noted that the six-tenths cloud he had found from 10,000 feet to 15,000 feet was gradually coming down to 4000 feet and covered most of north-east France.

His radar operator announced another contact and the Heinkel arrowed towards it, fastening on to a four-engined bomber at 0430 hours with the dawn beginning to come up faintly behind them. This time the kill was quick and the bomber crashed in flames, again in the Abbeville area.

Modrow continued his search, but finding no more victims he eventually turned on course for Venlo. The time was now 0600 hours, and the dawn was coming up fast.

He had just lowered his undercarriage for landing when he saw the ghostly outline of a Mosquito as it swept low over the Venlo airfield. Before touching down, he quickly alerted ground control: and seconds later the Mosquito screamed through the mist on a dead-straight course for England. Modrow, who now lives at Goch, says, "I assumed that he had completed his mission and flew low on his return flight so as to draw as little attention as possible."

Up to this time, Modrow had already shot down one British aircraft but had not been officially credited with it. "I can only remember," he says, "that this unrecognised shooting-down of my first aircraft took place during the night we lost the two aces Meurer and Wittgenstein, who up to then had been our most successful night-fighters. It was some time during mid-January nineteen forty-four."

As far as he was able to tell, he was the only pilot from Venlo to bring down a bomber on the night of the Nuremberg action.

The fighter snaked in on Squadron Leader Creswell's Pathfinder Lancaster B-Beer north-west of Paris. And in the split second of sighting it, his tail-gunner rapped an order over the intercom for a corkscrew to port. Creswell immediately banked the heavy aircraft, slammed the wheel forward and jammed on left rudder . . . and then a sixth sense, born of long experience in piloting a bomber through the hell-spots of the Third Reich, prompted him to suddenly reverse the manoeuvre. Whipping the Lancaster into a starboard dive, he was in time to see a stream of tracer shells zip across the patch of sky out of which he had just twisted. Had he gone on with his port dive, the tracer would have hosed right through the aircraft.

As the Lancaster lurched downwards, its crew experienced a series of loud and alarming bangs which could have been the repercussion of bursting shells or a buffeting from the slip-stream of the fighter or . . . No one could tell for certain. All that Creswell knew was that his control column had gone slack and mushy: and he felt the bomber dropping like a lift. For a moment, he had the uneasy notion that their tail had been shot off. Ahead he could see the Channel – silent, dark and deep . . . freedom, if they could make it.

He fought the controls and the bomber responded; but through his forward panel he could see the fighter curving in for another attack. It would be ironic, he thought, if after all they had been through they were shot down so near to home.

As he dropped the Lancaster's nose the fighter flashed over them, the black crosses on its wings looking incredibly huge. Creswell twisted round in his seat and watched it as it flipped over in a left-hand turn for a port beam attack. Then, as it flattened out to line the bomber in its gun-sights, he turned sharply into the attack with cool precision and thwarted the attempt. This he followed by hauling B-Beer into a tight corkscrew. His timing was perfect. When he rolled the Lancaster out of its dive there was no sign of their attacker.

But B-Beer had not come out of the duel unscathed. A direct hit had been scored on one of its petrol tanks, and Creswell knew it was a miracle that the bomber had not exploded. Now they needed another miracle, for he very much doubted that there was enough fuel left with which to reach their base.

As if things were not bad enough, mist and fog now en-

gulfed them in swirling eddies. It was time, Creswell decided, to send out an S.O.S. But so many emergency calls
were being transmitted by other helpless bombers that no
one seemed to take any notice of his wireless-operator's
Mayday distress signals.

By now, knowing beyond doubt that they could never
make their own base, Creswell was ready to land anywhere; and so he headed for the nearest coastal airfield –
the Fleet Air Arm station at Ford. There was really no
option. It was a landing at Ford – or nowhere. And when he
reached the field there was again no option. There simply
wasn't enough fuel for circling first: it had to be a straight,
flat approach.

"We left a rather badly damaged aircraft on the runway,"
he wrote afterwards, "with a burst tyre, half the elevator
shot off and a hole one could crawl through in the port
wing. Why she didn't blow up I shall never know. I found
out later that a cannon shell had lodged in the armour-
plating of my seat, the firing pin having been bent over
during its passage through the fuselage . . . How lucky can
one be?"

Of the intuitive flash he'd had in ignoring his gunner's
call to corkscrew to port when the fighter attacked them,
Creswell says, "It just goes to show how thin one's life-
thread is. I suddenly thought that the bastards always
reckoned on one turning to port, so I whipped the aircraft
over to starboard."

Chapter Seventeen

The surviving bombers droned on through the storm which had been mercilessly flailing and mauling them ever since leaving Nuremberg, until ahead in the dawn light crews could see the blurred outline of the Channel coast. Navigators now noted that the wind was dropping with each air mile, and hopes rose as the storm suddenly passed them and the weather cleared as if by magic.

The calm that follows battle-fatigue caressed the men. They were nearly home, and a new day was beginning. Bomb-aimers left their H2S sets, their job long since done, and lumbered into the noses of the bombers to see the birth of a sunrise they hadn't dared to think about during the long night of death and destruction. But they, like everyone else aboard, were to be bitterly disappointed. As unexpectedly as the weather had changed for the better, it now changed again for the worse. Only this time it was a different menace that faced the crews – writhing banks of flat, grey, dense fog, stretching before them like an impenetrable wall.

Spirits that had risen with the tantalisingly brief spell of clear weather rapidly sagged again. There seemed to be no end to the night of hell. Visibility was down to zero – except where occasional gaps in the fog tops gave crews a glimpse of red-orange mushrooms of flame from badly damaged planes that simply fell from the sky to disintegrate on home soil. Everything seemed hopeless again.

Some crews were forced to abandon their shattered aircraft and bale out within a few miles of crossing the English coast, first turning their plane on a course which would take it out to sea – where it would eventually disappear without trace.

The air over half of England that foggy dawn hummed with Mayday calls as wireless-operators tapped out desperate emergency signals in the knowledge that they could not remain airborne much longer. And from control towers of fog-shrouded bases equally frantic signals flashed back to the bombers, diverting them to fog-free airfields where grim-faced controllers fought the clock to sort out landing priorities and get the flak-battered aircraft down as swiftly as possible on beam-landings.

Homing on Gee fixes was the order of the day as battle-scarred Lancasters and Halifaxes made fraught circuits over almost-invisible runways, waiting for the order to pancake; and for many crews, as they orbited with virtually empty fuel tanks, it was a more nerve-racking ordeal than any bomb-run they had ever made.

One circuiting Lancaster was D-Don of 156 Squadron, aboard which Sergeant Holley had been struggling to stay awake ever since leaving Nuremberg. He had vaguely heard his navigator's call that they had crossed the French coast before dropping off to sleep, and he had woken again after they had crossed the English coast. Now the tension of locating their landing field kept him awake and brought a new alertness to his tired brain.

Gradually, Squadron Leader Brooks brought the Lancaster down through thick cloud on to the course given him by his navigator for their base at Upwood. Flying Officer Jones then read off a new set of fixes from the Gee box and announced that they were over the base. The bomber was now down to nine hundred feet, but still the cloud was solid.

Brooks sliced off more height, until his altimeter showed that they were at three hundred feet, and told his crew that he would take the plane a bit lower to try to get under the cloud base. He could see nothing outside but thick, smothering vapour.

The Lancaster's engines increased their throbbing as if in protest as Jones, after taking another fix, warned that they were getting away from the base and gave his pilot a course alteration that would take them back over Upwood. They were now at a height of two hundred feet, and Brooks' right hand gripped the throttle levers firmly in readiness to give the engines more power should it be necessary to climb hurriedly. He fully realised the danger of attempting to fly lower with visibility nil, but there was no alternative.

"I'm not going to call up control," he told the crew. "They'll only divert us. Hang on and keep your fingers crossed."

He then slammed open his side-panel as an aid to vision – and was amazed to be showered with snow.

"Christ!" he shouted. "This isn't cloud . . . it's a bloody snowstorm! No wonder I can't see a thing. The blasted windscreen's covered with thick snow."

Moments later his voice came to them again, and though it was calm they detected in it an underlying tone of caution. "We're down to a hundred feet," he said. "We can't go much lower without hitting something, that's for sure."

He then dropped the port wing gently and peered out of the side-window in the hope of glimpsing the tall chimneys of an old brickworks that was near Upwood. But before he could take in anything his flight-engineer, Sergeant Sabin, called out that he thought he had seen some Drem lights (the guide-lights that mark the perimeter of an airfield) to their starboard.

Brooks hauled the Lancaster into a steep right-hand turn and saw the faint, flickering lights of Upwood: and in that instant the aircraft pitched wildly and Brooks froze in his seat as another Lancaster slid a few feet above them, blasting D-Don with its slipstream.

"Jee-zus!" someone gasped over the intercom. "Did you see that?"

They had seen it all right. Holley remembers, "We all

thought we'd had it." And he goes on to describe what happened next. "Brooks took the Lancaster down to seventy feet and ordered the engineer to drop the undercarriage. 'We'll follow the Drem lights round and swing on to the runway as soon as it shows up through this muck,' he announced. But it wasn't as simple as it sounded. On our first trip round we were too close and crossed the runway at right-angles. On our next circuit we missed it completely. I had my turret facing port and, when on our next orbit the engineer shouted 'Hard to port', Brooks banked so steeply that I found myself looking straight down at the deck.

"A moment later, he straightened D-Don and told us, 'O.K., I've got it . . . Stand by to cut engines . . . *Cut*!' The next moment we hit the tarmac with quite a thump. Brooks swung the aircraft sharply to face the direction from which we had landed. This rather unorthodox procedure had the effect of pulling us up more effectively – and more quickly – than any application of the brakes would have.

"Ours was the first and only aircraft to land at Upwood whilst the snow was falling. Half an hour later, when we had completed our interrogation of the raid, four more bombers from the squadron landed. The majority had called up earlier and had been diverted to other airfields.

"We soon learned how lucky we had been. Usually, one of the hottest spots on an operation was to be in the first wave – with the fighters doing their utmost to prevent the Pathfinders getting to the target and illuminating the aiming point. On this occasion we had been extremely fortunate in being in the role of primary markers. While I had seen a mere four or five aircraft going down as we flew south of the Ruhr, several of my colleagues who had been further back in the bomber stream were attacked. According to their count, over forty bombers had got the chop in that area.

"I doubt if I would have dozed so well on the way back had I realised things were so dicey. I was even more shaken when I heard that four of our own squadron Lancasters had gone down."

Shaken also were station commanders and de-briefing officers, some of whom dismissed as rubbish the aircrews' claims that this would prove to be the costliest raid ever.

The crew members of Lancaster Y-Yorker of No. 44 Squadron were among those who were told that they were talking nonsense. But even the final stage of their journey home was not without incident. As they neared the enemy coast they observed two anti-aircraft guns, about a mile apart, sending up cones of fire that crossed at 10,000 feet: and a few seconds later a bomber was caught in the cross-fire and fell in flames. Y-Yorker dived rapidly and cleared the coast at 100 feet.

Landing at their base at Dunholme Lodge on three en-gines, the crew went straight to the interrogation room where their flight-engineer, Flight Lieutenant Burrows, was surprised to see the imposing six-foot-six figure of their base commander, Air Commodore 'Poppy' Pope, standing beside the station commander, Group Captain Butler. Both of these officers asked the Flight Lieutenant how the operation had gone.

Recounts Burrows, "When I stated that I thought we had lost about a hundred aircraft I was told not to be ridiculous. They turned to the doctor and remarked, 'Send this crew on leave. It's time they had a rest.' The de-briefing was very quiet and the atmosphere was electric.

"It certainly appeared to me that Jerry was waiting for us, and there were rumours that the raid had been leaked. In fact, it was said quite openly during interrogation – with lots of derogatory remarks being made.

"We lost seven aircraft from our unit, and we noticed at breakfast that many seats were empty. I remember, too, that there were plenty of fried eggs to spare. They had been cooked for crews who never returned. That evening we consumed gallons of ale."

There was a firm belief among aircrews from other

squadrons that the Germans had known in advance that the target was to be Nuremberg. Flight Sergeant Gardner, wireless-operator in Lancaster D-Don of No. 103 Pathfinder Squadron, says, "Everyone I talked to after the raid was sure that it had been leaked. As a Pathfinder aircraft, we were normally with the lead bombers and seldom were we attacked by fighters until well into Germany. But this time they met us at the coast in force. I saw more gathered there than at any time in my tour of operations."

Of the atmosphere at de-briefing, Gardner goes on to say, "The crews were anti-Met and very angry at both the route and the weather forecasts we had been given. New crews were severely shaken.

"People did not realise that our actual losses from raids were very much heavier than were ever given out, because aircraft that returned shot-up and crashed in England were not counted in the bulletins given to the public. There were many that night who made it back but didn't live to tell about it."

But as more bombers touched down and their crews were interrogated, station commanders began to realise that the loss rate was indeed likely to be appalling. Clocks on briefing-room walls were watched anxiously, and there was mounting unease at the number of blank spaces on squadron operation-boards indicating crews that had failed to return. And now the aircrews that had come back were questioned with a new urgency.

As Sergeant Rowlinson, wireless-operator of Lancaster H-Harry of No. 50 Squadron, recalls, "The de-briefing took much longer than was usual. Of the fourteen aircraft that took off from our squadron only eight returned: and the interrogation officers particularly questioned the gunners. They wanted to know everything – the times and positions of combats, and the manner in which aircraft went down. Not only were the individual crews alarmed, but also the top brass. They seemed to think that slackness on the part of the aircrews was to blame for a large percentage of the losses. The immediate result was a general tightening up on discipline and an increase in 'bull', which did not go down at all well with the crews.

"Apart from the bright moonlight, I think fatigue played a big part in the Nuremberg casualty rates. The mental and physical strain of operating every other night was very much greater than was realised at the time by both the individual and the authorities."

Flight Sergeant Frank Wildman, D.F.M., who now lives in Bridlington, was the flight-engineer in Lancaster R-Robert, a Pathfinder of No. 83 Squadron, stationed at Wyton. The aircraft was a visual-marker and it reached the target area without being attacked by night-fighters; but the crew saw many bombers going down in flames behind them. Navigator Flying Officer Davidson counted over fifty of them before the pilot, Flight Lieutenant Hellier, told him to stop logging them and concentrate on his navigation instead.

"We were one of the first aircraft over Nuremberg," Wildman has written, "and the target was not particularly 'hot' at that stage, as far as we were concerned. In fact, we thought it rather quiet on the bomb-run after having done eleven sorties to Berlin during the previous month. But we felt that something was really happening behind us. This made us a bit apprehensive about the return trip, yet it turned out to be uneventful.

"As we neared Wyton we were diverted because of fog to Downham Market, where an estimated seven squadrons landed. There were all sorts of rumours flying about, but no official explanation was ever given to us for the high losses. We were one of the first aircraft to land at Downham Market so there was not a hint at our de-briefing of the large numbers of bombers that had not returned. Crews who landed there could not be sure how their squadrons had fared because of the number of diversions. The shock came in the morning when the official figures were announced."

Chapter Eighteen

Master-Pathfinder Wing Commander Pat Daniels of No. 35 P.F.F. Squadron was the first to land at Graveley, to find Air Vice-Marshal Bennett waiting for him in the de-briefing room. Bennett, who usually drove over from his head-quarters in nearby Huntingdon to greet his Pathfinders on their return from an operation and receive their accounts of the action, was particularly anxious for first-hand news of the Nuremberg raid. And he was about to get it in no uncertain terms.

Daniels, normally a good-humoured officer, was angry and bitter. "Bloody hell! Why did we have to go that way?" he demanded of his chief, going on to express his opinion of the route much as he had before the raid and adding that, whether by luck or design, there had been more fighter attacks than on any other operation he had been on.

Bennett was fully aware that there were few better or braver pilots than Daniels in the whole of Bomber Command, and he had always got on very well with him. He therefore took no exception to the outburst, trying rather to calm the man down as best he could. But Daniels was not to be mollified. In all of his experience, he told Bennett, he had never seen so many bombers going down – so many, he stressed, that he had told his navigator not to attempt the impossible task of logging them.

At first Bennett was inclined to be sceptical, not wanting to believe that the operation could have been such a disaster. But he knew that Daniels was not the type of man to exaggerate an action – the D.S.O. and double D.F.C.s on his battledress were a mute testament to his record – and neither was he likely to allow battle-fatigue to cloud his judgment. And so Bennett, who had himself protested vigorously against the straight route to Nuremberg during the previous morning's briefing, began to fear the worst – finding empty consolation in the knowledge that his proposed alternative route had been thrown out by the main-force commanders.

Of his conversation with Bennett, Daniels says, "To appease me he took me over to the big wall map and, while I drank my tea from a dirty cup – it still tasted very good after seven and a half hours flying – he talked of the future targets in the south of Germany, which had so far been untouched. He pointed out to me, in confidence, the targets we would have to attack there and explained that they were lightly defended.

"There were some big ones which would have to be done soon, he said. Munich was one of them – and it was finally done successfully. However, I thought the difficulty after this night's show would be to get there – especially in bright moonlight. We had climbed that night through cloud over the sea, and when we got above it there was bright moonlight. Although there was thick cloud over the target, it was the brightest moonlight I can remember flying in.

"I again stressed to Bennett that on this raid there was a large number of sightings of aircraft blowing up. Most of them were brought down by fighters. There was also a large number of scare-shells sent up to simulate an aircraft exploding – and they were very good imitations. But I soon found out that in many cases they were, in fact, bombers blowing up. The fighter attacks on the bombers usually started a small fire in the fuselage or wing, which was spread by the slip-stream and wind to the fuel tanks and bombs. Then everything went up. Often, though, it was difficult to be sure whether it was a bomber exploding or a scare-shell."

Commenting on the route, Daniels continues, "I can't

think why they sent us on a straight line. Bennett usually had the right to send his group of Pathfinders by any route he chose. They did not often take the same route as the main force, and they normally arrived about ten minutes before them. We used to make spoof raids on different targets close to the actual one we were to bomb about five minutes before the raid was due to open, in the hope that the fighters would go there and concentrate their watch on the spoof one. Then we'd turn right or sharp left to the real target.

"The inexperienced crews bombed short, so we used to put our markers right at the far end of the target. People had a tendency, when they saw all the flak and searchlights, to drop their bombs quickly and get the hell out of it – so that raids always tended to creep back.

"As master bomber, we would arrive five minutes before anybody else. It was extremely unpleasant. Sometimes the Germans would all stay quiet, hoping that you were just a stray aircraft and thinking that if they didn't open up you'd pass on. But later, when they knew our technique, they would concentrate on trying to shoot down the first air-craft that arrived – as they did on Nuremberg.

"With Bennett, of course, you weren't allowed just to carry flares: you had to have bombs, whatever else you were carrying."

Although Daniels had heard the rumour that the Germans knew in advance of the Nuremberg operation, he did not believe it. He points out now that, with the exception of the Dieppe operation, the functioning of the security forces of all three services was top rate. "On days of opera-tions, after briefings, no private telephone calls were allowed to any personnel either in or out of camp," he says. "Although the target was usually known to the operational-room staff and the station and squadron commanders, the aircrews did not learn of it until briefing; and the ground-crews did not know where we had been until we returned from the operation."

This, of course, was the general rule throughout Bomber Command's operational stations – and it was rigidly applied. It is therefore extraordinary that one R.A.F. officer – Squadron Leader Philip R. Goodwin of No. 156 Pathfinder Squadron, who was shot down in the Nuremberg action – claimed that after the briefing for the operation he made a telephone call to his wife from his base at Upwood to tell her that he had arrived back safely from leave. Goodwin's theory that the attack was in fact betrayed appeared some years ago in the German magazine *Neue Illustrierte* in an article by David Irving, author of *The Destruction of Dresden*. Mr. Irving reported that the Squadron Leader was sure that espionage had been involved.

According to the article, Goodwin—like many of the aircrews who had flown against Nuremberg – had been astonished at the number of bombers he saw going down. But it was not until his bomb-aimer remarked that the Germans could not have shot down more if they had planned the course themselves or had foreknowledge of the raid that Goodwin remembered the telephone call he had made to his wife. Not that he had been in any way indiscreet.

In common with many others that night, Goodwin had believed that the raid would eventually be cancelled because of the weather. And he had been even more convinced of this when his station switchboard put his call through. As a senior officer, he was well aware of the ruling on private telephone calls after a briefing. The fact that he had been permitted to make one seemed a tacit admission that there would be no raid.

When he got through to his wife he made no mention of the fact that he might be on operations that night, merely telling her that he'd had a good leave and was looking forward to his next one. But the fact that there'd been a lapse in security that had enabled him to telephone his wife came back to him when he learned the number of aircraft lost in the Nuremberg venture, and the explanation seemed obvious. If there had been one lapse, there could have been another . . . and their destination must have been known in advance. A German agent on the base could have passed information on the target and the course the bombers were to fly to a contact outside, who in turn could have relayed it to German Intelligence.

Irving's article went on to record that Goodwin's Path-finder Lancaster had been attacked and that the Squadron Leader had baled out from the burning bomber. Two days after being taken prisoner, Goodwin – still according to Irving – met another captured British airman who told him that a German Intelligence officer had remarked, while questioning him on 30th March 1944, that Nuremberg was to be attacked that night at midnight. On his return to Britain after the war, Goodwin reported his suspicions to the Royal Air Force.

And Goodwin was not the only R.A.F. prisoner-of-war to have heard the rumour in captivity. Roy Macdonald, a former mid-upper gunner now of Maidenhead, was another.

Macdonald, who flew with No. 35 Squadron, was shot down after a raid on Krefeld on 21st June 1943. In a personal communication, he tells that while he was in Stalag Luft VI he met an airman who had been shot down on a raid just before the Nuremberg operation. This airman asserted that he had been sent to the Frankfurt interrogation centre on 30th March 1944 and, while being questioned during the morning, had been told by the Germans that Bomber Command was going to attack Nuremberg that night.

There is no doubt in Macdonald's mind that the man he spoke to was a genuine R.A.F. man and not a trained German impersonating one to gain his confidence and wheedle information from him. He is also absolutely convinced that the airman – whose name and squadron he cannot recall after so many years – had not invented the story. The conversation was first brought back to him shortly afterwards when he and his fellow prisoners-of-war heard a B.B.C. news bulletin on the Nuremberg raid over a secret radio-receiver they had made.

Asked recently if, on looking back on the conversation, he still thought it probable that the Germans could have told the airman in advance of the raid, Macdonald replied, "I don't see why not. As far as I could gather, the Germans had an excellent Intelligence system. Their knowledge of individual squadrons – their location and personnel – was quite remarkable. This, of course, was probably obtained from interrogation and from papers and photographs carried by careless airmen who had disobeyed orders and taken these things with them. No one taking part in raids would be able to give information on pending ones as they would not know the target until a few hours before the operation.

"However, the Germans obviously had an espionage system operating in Britain during the war and it would appear feasible that occasionally they might get hold of a spot of advance information from somewhere concerning a raid. In any case, the losses on Nuremberg were so abnormal that I am sure most people genuinely thought it had been leaked."

The Germans certainly knew about most of the top R.A.F. bomber squadron commanders. Wing Commander Daniels says, "They knew a lot about me: not only my war record but also my social activities. And they used to bring up all sorts of details concerning my squadron when they interrogated new prisoners. Unfortunately, some prisoners no doubt did divulge information after they had fallen for confidence tricks or were subjected to physical threats. It was rumoured at the time that the raid was leaked, but on the whole our security was excellent."

It could well be that the airman Macdonald had talked to was the innocent victim of a confidence trick on the part of the intelligence officer who had interrogated him. In the period that had elapsed between being shot down, captured and eventually questioned, his sense of time might easily have been confused. It would then have been comparatively simple for a skilled intelligence officer to bluff him into believing that Nuremberg was going to be attacked when in fact the raid had already taken place. This would have had the effect of softening him up for further questioning, giving him the impression that his interrogators already knew all the answers.

That it was a piece of bluff attempted by an interrogating officer is the view of the Air Ministry, having discovered no German records to confirm that details of the Nuremberg raid were known in advance.

There was, in fact, not much difference between the British and German methods of interrogation. Macdonald recalls, "In the little cells at Frankfurt, I was interrogated first of all by one very bland German who gave me a bogus Red Cross form to fill in with practically everything on it – your civilian occupation, how much pay you got, what your grandmother's name was, and everything else. He was most hurt when I did not give him anything other than my name, rank and number. He told me, 'You have not filled in civilian occupation.' I replied that he would not be interested in that, and he said, 'I don't know. I think possibly you were an important designer.' When I asked what made him think that, he replied that I had a very important crew, there being two flight lieutenants in it.

"He went on to tell me, 'You've no need to try and keep anything from me. I know you've come from 35 P.F.F. Squadron at Graveley and that you have a C.O. named Robinson.' I said, 'Oh, well – that's very interesting, I'm sure.' He then left me.

"They had letters, photographs and other things of people off the squadron and they could tell from these the name of the local bit of stuff down in the village, and the local taxi-driver's name; but more than that, I was shown a photostat of a letter regarding the formation of the Path-finder Force. It was addressed to the C.O. of 35 Squadron. Now presumably, on the formation of the Pathfinders in August nineteen forty-two, one of these letters must have been sent to each squadron. I was shown the one that was

sent to ours. Where it came from, heaven alone knows. We used to empty our pockets completely, except for money, before we took off; but some clots did carry photographs and letters."

The Germans treated their R.A.F. aircrew prisoners well, and no brutality was used during interrogation. But Macdonald recalls that it could be a different story if a member of a bombing crew was caught by civilians during or immediately after a raid on their town or city. He says, "I remember a Flight Lieutenant Sachs, whom I met as a prisoner-of-war. He was the rear-gunner of a bomber that was shot down during the Battle of Hamburg. The civilians got him and as he was the senior member of the crew, they assumed he was the pilot. They gave him a hell of a beating . . . They took off his boots and then proceeded to hammer his face in with them. He was still sort of jumpy when I met him. He told me that they then took him out to a lorry in which there were five or six dead R.A.F. aircrew and drove him through the outskirts of Hamburg where he said there was a body hanging up at virtually every intersection. I don't suppose you could blame the Germans really. There were a lot of people in England who felt pretty much the same."

It is true that civilians of any nation subjected to the ferocity of a mass saturation bombing raid could not be expected to look upon their exterminators as anything but cold-blooded murderers and would be apt to react to the hysteria of the moment; but nevertheless, there is no record of the manhandling of any of the bomber crews that baled out over Nuremberg.

As to the question of whether or not the Nuremberg raid could have been leaked, it is worth considering the following extract from a Minute to the Prime Minister from Air Marshal Sir Arthur Harris, dated 2nd May 1942 and published in the official British history of the strategic air offensive against Germany:

I could not in any circumstances agree to discuss projected attacks outside my Headquarters with other departments. I do not even tell my crews, to whom security is a matter of life and death, where they are going until the last possible moment before briefing. I am sure indeed that a continuation of that policy is the first essential of security. You, as C.A.S., are the only people who ever know my intended precise targets prior to the day, except in special cases, such as the Tirpitz operation, wherein other departments have to be consulted about such things as special weapons.

The late Sir Robert Saundby discounted the rumour in personal conversations about the Nuremberg operation shortly before his death. "Our Intelligence were never able to discover any evidence that the Germans knew where we were going on any occasion," he said, "and I do not think they ever did. The proof of this is that we were able, so often, to spoof them. We had a fully-manned German control room after the war and we worked out our spoofs with them and it was clear that they never knew where we were going.

"We also had a big Corona station in Kent. Corona was the code-word for a successful deception we used to work on the German night-fighter and ground defences. Through it we confused their night-fighter and ground defences by using fluent German-speaking personnel. These people would broadcast from our powerful monitoring station at Kingsdown in Kent giving false instructions to the night-fighter crews and ground defences. They also sent out wrong weather reports to the German night-fighters, telling them that bad weather or fog was coming in and ordering them to land.

"Our German-speakers were very skilful and could mimic the German controllers they were impersonating. They used to pretend that they were the authentic controllers and inferred that it was the real Germans who were giving the fighters confusing and inaccurate instructions. When in their frustration the German controllers started swearing and cursing at our Corona operators, they would retort, 'Oh listen! The Englishman is swearing now!' I am convinced from what the German controllers told me at the end of the war that they never knew what target Bomber Command was heading for."

What finally seems to make nonsense of the rumour is the fact that had German Intelligence foreknowledge that Nuremberg was to be attacked General Josef Schmid, chief of the supreme command for the air defence of Germany, would have been immediately alerted. Yet Schmid, as has already been seen, did not have a clue as to where the main attack would be and had to plot the course of the bombers with wariness before ordering the first of his night-fighter squadrons to take off.

Neither had the German night-fighter pilots any idea that there was to be a raid that night. Many of them, as their own statements disclose, did not even seriously consider that Bomber Command would operate on a night when the weather was so favourable to visual interception.

Nevertheless, the rumour persisted – and persists even today – among those with an academic interest in aerial warfare as well as aircrews who attacked Nuremberg on that disastrous night.

Chapter Nineteen

Sir Robert Saundby had much to brood over in his office in 'Springfield', the country-house headquarters of Sir Arthur Harris, during the bleak early hours of 31st March 1944. The first of the returning bombers had landed at their bases at about 0433 hours, the last of them at 0652 hours: and some hadn't made it at all – surviving the raid only to crash in the sea or somewhere in England. But as details of the squadrons' losses flowed into Bomber Command Headquarters it was already clear beyond any shadow of doubt that the 'missing' rate would be in the region of 11.8 per cent – an all-time peak figure (never to be surpassed at any later stage of the air-war against Germany or, for that matter, in any other air action anywhere).

The significance of it can only be fully appreciated when that percentage is seen in relation to previous losses. There had been concern, for instance, over the cost in aircrew and aircraft of the Battle of Berlin. In six operations mounted on the German capital in January 1944, the 'missing' rate had been 6.1 per cent. During the same month it rose to 7.2 per cent in actions against Stettin, Brunswick and Magdeburg. And in the following month, February, it soared to the even higher level of 9.5 per cent when seventy-eight aircraft were lost in an attack on Leipzig.

The expenditure in terms of experienced airmen was frightening. Every bomber crew had to do thirty operations before being rested – and 'rested' meant instructing at operational training units, where the accident rate was high. Pathfinder crews were required to do a double tour of operations – sixty raids over Germany. With a five per cent casualty rate, the mathematical odds against survival were three to one. And Saundby, studying the chilling incoming reports, was painfully aware that a casualty rate of five per cent was about as much as any bomber force could stand over a period of time. The losses in the Nuremberg raid were therefore truly appalling.

There was hardly a squadron that had not suffered to some extent, and there were many – like No. 101 Squadron on special duties – that were grievously mauled. Of the twenty-six aircraft of No. 101 Squadron that took off for the raid fitted with special radio equipment for jamming and confusing night-fighter radio communications, six failed to return and one crashed near Newbury, killing the entire crew.

In its final analysis of the cost of the most disastrous raid in its history, Bomber Command found that of the 795 aircraft sent against Nuremberg only 616 actually attacked the city. Many of the others had been forced to bomb last-resort targets such as Schweinfurt, Ansbach, West Kapelle, Flushing and Erlangen – to little or no effect.

The action report sent to Command Headquarters read as follows:

No. 1 Group: 181 aircraft from Nos. 12, 100, 101, 103, 166, 460, 550, 576, 625 and 626 Squadrons were detailed for the raid, and of these 180 took off. 142 attacked the primary target, 8 the last-resort target, 8 were abortive, 21 failed to return and 1 crashed.

No. 3 Group: 59 aircraft from Nos. 15, 75, 90, 115, 149, 199, 514 and 622 Squadrons were detailed, and 56 took off. Of these 7 returned early and 49 attacked, of which 8 failed to return.

No. 4 Group: 138 aircraft from Nos. 10, 51, 76, 78, 158, 466, 578 and 640 Squadrons were detailed, of which 121 took off. 76 attacked the primary target, 21 were abortive, 20 failed to return and 3 crashed.

No. 5 Group: 203 aircraft from Nos. 9, 44, 49, 50, 57, 61, 207, 463, 467, 617, 619 and 630 Squadrons detailed, of which 201 took off. 11 returned early, 159 attacked the primary target, 10 attacked the last-resort target. 21 failed to return.

No. 6 Group: 120 aircraft from Nos. 408, 420, 424, 425, 426, 427, 429, 432 and 433 Squadrons detailed, of which 118 took off, 8 returned early, 94 attacked the primary target, 3 the alternative target. 13 failed to return.

No. 8 Group: 122 detailed. 119 aircraft took off from Squad-
(PFF)   rons No. 7, 35, 83, 97, 105, 139, 156, 405, 582, 627 and 692. Of these 96 attacked Nuremberg, 6 returned early and 11 failed to return.

There was one bright note in the report – No. 8 Group attacked ten other targets that night with fifty-one Mosquitos, all of which returned. The operation report was as follows:

Aachen: 6 Mosquitos took off, 5 successfully attacked and 1 attack was abortive. Kassel: 19 Mosquitos took off and all attacked. Cologne: 9 Mosquitos attacked, but two of the attacks were abortive. Twente airfield was attacked by 4 Mosquitos, 3 of them successful; while 9 Mosquitos raided the airfields at Volkel, Deelen, Juvincourt and Julianadorf.

But the rest of the report made dismal reading. Fifty bombers were destroyed between Aachen and the turning point at Fulda, all of them by night-fighters. Three were shot down on the approach to Nuremberg, five more over the target, and four on the return journey. Fourteen were brought down by flak, and two collided over the target and were seen to go down in flames. This accounted for a total of seventy-eight of the ninety-four losses.

In addition to the ninety-four, seventeen aircraft received minor flak damage and thirty-four were damaged by fighters – three beyond unit repair and four beyond any kind of repair. Five were damaged by incendiaries falling from bombers above them, one being a complete write-off, and fifteen were damaged by other than enemy action – of which seven were written-off and two were wrecked beyond unit repair. These included aircraft damaged when landing.

Thus a total of seventy-one valuable aircraft, out of the seven hundred and ninety-five despatched, suffered varying degrees of damage.

There are no readily accessible records to show the number of bases where it was impossible for bombers to land because of fog, but it appears that at least seven aircraft were lost over England while trying to find a landing place – and that is considered a very conservative estimate.

Although 2,460 tons of bombs were dropped between 0105 hours and 0122 hours, there was no photographic evidence to show that any of them fell in the target area. Indeed, there was insufficient photographic evidence to reconstruct the course of the raid in detail. But what little there was clearly showed that the bombing was spread widely downwind to the east of the target. Furthermore, because of the high winds that dispersed the sky-markers, the bombing was poorly concentrated.

In its summing-up of the raid, Bomber Command was forced to concede that the German night-fighters had achieved a considerable success. Massed in two groups, near Bonn and Frankfurt, they had easily intercepted the bomber stream and had conducted a running battle over a distance of nearly two hundred and fifty miles eastwards from Aachen. And only seven enemy fighters, it was estimated, were destroyed in combat with the bombers before the target was reached.

It wasn't until much later on the day of their return – 31st March 1944 – that the aircrews who had flown against Nuremberg fully realised the magnitude of their losses. All that they needed to know was contained in the closing sentence of a terse thirty-nine-word communiqué from the Air Ministry broadcast by the B.B.C.:

Last night, aircraft of Bomber Command were over Germany in very great strength. The main objective was Nuremberg. Other aircraft attacked targets in western Germany, and mines were laid in enemy waters. Ninety-six of our aircraft are missing.

Chapter Twenty

In a subsequent communiqué, the Air Ministry amended the number of missing aircraft to ninety-four – but that took no account of the bombers that came down in the sea on the homeward flight or crashed in England before they could reach their bases. Such an oversight, however, is the least of the oddities concerning the Nuremberg operation.

Surely the strangest thing is that hardly a word about this incredible raid is to be found in the official records. Winston Churchill, in his mammoth history of World War 2, dismissed it in one short paragraph; and Harris, in his book on the bomber offensive published shortly after the war, surprisingly made no mention of it at all. In fact, Nuremberg is omitted from the map of principal German targets printed on the inside hard covers of his book, which nevertheless shows such obscure places as Trier, Worms, Soest, Paderborn and many others which were never at any time associated with big raids. Why such reticence?

And why Nuremberg, anyway? What did the city possess to warrant a huge force flying a long and perilous distance at a time of year when the nights were getting shorter? Apart from the large Siemens Electric works, there were only a few light-engineering factories there.

To Churchill, however, Nuremberg was the living symbol of Nazism. It was more closely associated with Hitler's regime than any other city in Germany. The beer-cellars of Munich had spawned the party, but it was here that the infamous Nuremberg Laws – the series of anti-Semitic edicts – were promulgated. And it was here, too, that the

Nazi Party held its yearly congress. One can well understand, therefore, that the obliteration of Nuremberg would be seen by Churchill as being of immense propaganda value throughout the free world. Did he, then, order the raid? It would have been in character, for he had warned Italy shortly after she had entered the war that one day the long arm of Bomber Command would reach out over her cities: and as he had promised, British bombs did fall on Milan and Turin.

But Churchill, in his aforementioned history, gives no hint as to why Nuremberg was singled out for attack at that stage of the war. His reference to the raid is, indeed, remarkably brief. In Volume V, 'Closing the Ring', he does, however, make one significant comment: "This was our heaviest loss in one raid, and caused Bomber Command to re-examine its tactics before launching further deep-penetration attacks by night into Germany."

What went wrong at Nuremberg? Why did the raid become an utter shambles? And what strategically important target warranted the attentions of nearly eight hundred valuable Lancasters and Halifaxes and their crews?

Considering that it turned out to be Bomber Command's blackest of nights, with an unsurpassed slaughter of aircrews, it is astonishing that both Churchill and Harris left these questions unanswered in their memoirs.

Equally unforthcoming were the official historians commissioned to compile the history of the Royal Air Force in the Second World War. Sir Charles Webster and Noble Frankland, in *The Strategic Air Offensive Against Germany, 1939-1945* (Volume III), have given the action little more than a page in nearly a million words about the air war; and the official story of the Royal Air Force from 1939 to 1945 devotes even less space to the raid. Almost as an afterthought, the latter dispenses with the R.A.F.'s heaviest loss of the war as "a minor victory" for the German night-fighters – surely one of the classic understatements of war history.

But perhaps the Air Ministry was lulled into a false

appreciation of the magnitude and ferocity of the Nuremberg operation by evaluating the losses that night against the since-proved-mythical estimate of one hundred and eighty-five German aircraft claimed to have been shot down on 15th September 1940, when the Battle of Britain was at its height.

Some years ago, however, after that figure had been openly questioned, post-war research and detailed cross-checking of official German records having shown the actual German losses on 15th September 1940 to be fifty-six, the Air Ministry duly amended the previous figure. And at the same time, the date of the Germans' heaviest losses during the Battle of Britain was altered to 15th August 1940, when seventy-six aircraft were shot down. But the blanket of security shrouding the Nuremberg action was not lifted to disclose an authentic accounting of the losses sustained by the R.A.F. in the operation.

The Strategic Air Offensive Against Germany, 1939-1945 records that ninety-five aircraft failed to return; but Volume III of *The Royal Air Force, 1939-1945* says that ninety-four were missing. In their sparse reference to the raid, the authors of the former comment, "This, indeed, was a curious operation." And they go on to conclude that the operation "suffered the ill consequences of unusually bad luck and uncharacteristically bad and unimaginative planning" – a scathing verdict that even today leads to sharp clashes of opinion between the then chief of Bomber Command and the official historians.

Regrettably, a lack of understanding of Harris's role in carrying the war into Germany has led to him being much maligned and often unjustifiably attacked and criticised over the years – in the face of which he has normally held himself aloof. Indeed, only once did he break his customary silence to answer a critic publicly. That was when Earl Attlee, the wartime deputy Prime Minister, made an astonishing and seemingly inexplicable attack on him in which he asserted that Harris might have concentrated more "on military targets". Tersely, Harris reminded Attlee that the bomber policy he was now castigating had been formulated and decided upon by the government of which he had been a leading member.

As to whether the bomber offensive against Germany was wasteful, inhuman and ineffective in shortening the war, as his critics assert, Harris answers:

"All war is inhuman. The bomber offensive was not designed by me. It was carried out by me. As for the effect of it, even the official history – which has been misinterpreted so largely – concludes that, far from being futile, the bomber offensive was decisive as the war-winning effort."

Only when this is fully understood can the mass raids on Germany be seen in their proper perspective. But even then, the question "Why Nuremberg?" would remain to be answered.

In the course of long personal talks on the Nuremberg action with the late Sir Robert Saundby, he admitted that he thought very little had been achieved by it. Sir Robert explained, "The weather conditions were so bad that the timing went completely wrong. The marking was bad and the main force was late. It was a thorough shambles and one of the few occasions when everything went wrong.

"Harris often played his hunches, and mostly they were right. But I think he took a chance on Nuremberg. He did not think that the wind would be as strong as the Met people reckoned. Therefore, it was very difficult to argue with him. I was surprised that Harris had decided to bomb Nuremberg in view of the weather forecast we had been given. I was surprised too at the straight run-in. There were none of the diversions which the crews had come to expect and which had proved so valuable in cutting our losses. Sometimes we would feint for a place and do some jinking on the way to throw the fighters off and make it difficult for them to get back into the bomber stream. But the morning conference, which was almost public in the sense that so many advisers were present, was not the occasion for me to argue with the C-in-C.

"I did, however, express my doubts about the route when I saw him alone. And I did not at all like the direct return route. After the straight run-in I thought this was particularly dangerous – for the bombers would clear the coast in daylight. Frankly, I wondered if it was worth while going on with the raid; and I said this to Harris. He thought for a moment, then grunted – and those knowing him will appreciate how effective his grunts could be. After a moment, he said, 'We will leave it until we see the afternoon Met report. The Met people should then have a better chart to work on.'"

Saundby went on to say, "In the morning we had been given forecast winds in the region of forty to fifty miles per hour. Later, we were told to expect wind-speeds of around eighty miles per hour. A general or an admiral had plenty of time to call off his battle plans, but with us time was always short. Our decisions, accordingly, were usually snap ones. I thought that if the wind-speed had remained as was forecast in the morning we could just about do it, but there was no margin for error. If the wind got stronger, we would be in trouble. I had no doubt about that – just as I had no doubt, either, that Harris was playing a hunch.

"As it turned out, there were times on the flight out when the force had behind them winds of ninety miles an hour. It was one of the highest winds ever encountered by a bombing force; and they had to battle against them on the way back, when they were tired and battle-weary."

But Saundby was emphatic that no other form of attack could have been used that night. "We were not such fools as the official history suggests," he continued. "The straight flight plan seemed the lesser of the two evils. Had we allowed for dog-legging, we would have been caught in broad daylight over Germany because of the flying time that would have been wasted. With the distance the bombers had to go and the strength of the wind, we considered we had no alternative once it had been decided that the operation was to go on."

Sir Robert always believed that there were three reasons for his chief going ahead with the raid. The first, he said, was the pressure put on him by Churchill. "Churchill, as was well known, often interfered with his generals and admirals," he explained, "and I always had the impression that he exerted pressure on Harris to make this raid before Bomber Command was switched to the Overlord operations and attacks on pre-invasion targets in France. Nuremberg was the place where Hitler held his big rallies, and Churchill was persistent in that it must be bombed. And there was not much time, because the actual date of the switch-over to French targets had been fixed long before this raid. Air Chief Marshal Sir Arthur Tedder was the Deputy Supreme Allied Commander to Eisenhower, and Bomber Command was completely at his disposal for the Overlord operation. We knew that once we were turned over to Overlord it would be a long time before we would have another chance of attacking German cities."

Harris had strong views on Overlord – the code-name for the invasion of Europe by the Allies. He wanted no part of it. But as the planning of the invasion went ahead, it became clear to the Air Commander-in-Chief of the Allied Expeditionary Air Force Leigh-Mallory and his advisers that the air power at their disposal for Overlord was not great enough. At that time Leigh-Mallory had available to him the Second Tactical Air Force of the R.A.F., the United States Ninth Air Force and the R.A.F.'s Fighter Command – but he had no control over the United States Strategic Air Forces and Bomber Command, which remained under the Combined Chiefs of Staff.

When it was first proposed that Bomber Command should be switched to Overlord, Harris objected strongly. He was opposed to having his bombers fly ahead of an army to assault targets of its selection, arguing that they would be more effective assisting Overlord by continuing their bombing attacks on German cities and towns and disrupting industrial centres. Bomber Command was equipped and trained for just that, he contended, and it would be a grave error to use it instead for the bombing of beach defences, gun emplacements, ammunition dumps and communications.

He was not alone in so thinking, for there was at the time an influential body of opinion proclaiming that the war could be won without invading Europe. General Spaatz, commanding the United States Strategic Air Forces in Europe, backed Harris: and their stand was reinforced by the failure of the Allied Forces to take advantage of the bombing of Cassino, in Italy, in March 1944.

But Leigh-Mallory persisted; and despite Harris's vigorous opposition to a policy that he believed would lead to a serious misuse of his force, Bomber Command was switched to the bombing of invasion targets and railway centres in northern France. (In the event, results proved the soundness of Leigh-Mallory's plan – for the severe damage inflicted on railway tracks, engine sheds, repair centres and rolling stock forced the Germans to turn to road transport, with all the delays it involved.)

Thus it was the imminent transference of Bomber Command to Overlord that Saundby believed to be the second reason for the attack on Nuremberg at that particular time.

The third reason, he thought, was that the nights were growing shorter and there would therefore be fewer opportunities for launching deep-penetration raids into Germany.

Few people knew Harris better than Saundby, who had been a flight commander under him; and over the years Saundby had witnessed the successes his chief had had in backing his hunches. So he had no doubt that a hunch had motivated the go-ahead for Nuremberg.

"Harris was under pressure to make the attack," he said, "and he took a chance and backed a hunch. Had the weather been no worse than the Met forecast, he might have got away with it. But the odds were against us. The planning was not satisfactory – but that was due to circumstances and not to carelessness or lack of thought. In fact, the plan gave us more headaches than usual. The fear of a loss rate like the Nuremberg one was always with us. Every time we committed the force over Germany there was always the possibility of a disaster. There always is in war."

Sir Ralph Cochrane, who commanded No. 5 Group and who later became an Air Marshal, is also emphatic that no other type of attack could have been made against Nuremberg. In personal communications from his home at Bladon Castle, Burton-on-Trent, Sir Ralph – an outstandingly capable tactician who was detailed by Harris to organise the operation that breached the Moehne and Eder dams – comments:

"I cannot recall what route was put up by the Pathfinders, but for the main-force commanders to suggest an alternative one implies that it included features they could not accept. If these features were jinking or tactical trickery, I can understand their opposition. The stream of aircraft on the Nuremberg raid was anything up to fifty miles wide, and to throw off the fighters it would have been necessary to make a considerable turn – more than forty-five degrees – and hold it for at least half an hour, followed by a ninety-degree turn back.

"In practice, all this would have achieved would have been to lengthen the time to the target and therefore increase the risk of interceptions. On a long flight to the target, the tactical devices – whether by alterations of course or by diversionary attacks – were very limited, in a way which did not apply to short penetrations."

While agreeing with the part of the official historians' statement that says the raid "suffered the ill consequences of unusually bad luck", Sir Ralph strongly dissents with the concluding part of the sentence – "and uncharacteristically bad and unimaginative operational planning". In defence of his opinion, he goes on to say, "It is hard to see that any other routing would necessarily have been better. It had been general experience that the German night-fighter force was most likely to catch up with the bombers as they approached the target and during the early stages of the withdrawal. It was therefore better that this should take place away from and not towards the fighter bases – for example, as in the Nuremberg attack.

"The criticism of the long straight run-in is also open to question, for it will be noted that the German fighters had no difficulty in following the force when it turned south-east, near Fulda. Any other turns introduced – say, towards Frankfurt – would only have slowed down the rate of approach, without any indication that it would have thrown the fighters off the track.

"One has to remember, of course, that by the time it was opposite Frankfurt the bomber stream was probably fifty miles across. The plain fact was that it was too bright a night and the penetration was such that once the night-fighters had made contact they kept in the stream and made visual sightings. The point at which they first made contact was some hundred and fifty miles from the Dutch coast, which was a reasonable distance; but the force had then another two hundred miles to go. This was too far in the conditions of light that prevailed. The attack marked the greatest operational strength and efficiency of the German night force at a time when, except on dark nights, they had achieved an ascendancy over the night bomber.

"The Nuremberg attack was a failure, but with the then strength of the night-fighter force, the clear night and the deep penetration I doubt whether any other tactical approach would have achieved a very different result. It was fortunate for Bomber Command that the campaign in France kept it busy over the following months so that by the time it returned to distant targets in Germany conditions had much improved, leading to the victory which was decisive."

Whatever may be said of the merits or demerits of the route to and from Nuremberg, the diversions laid on in the past by Pathfinder Headquarters had invariably been successful.

A typical Pathfinder route made provision for a small but effective force of Mosquitos to fly ahead of the main bomber stream and attack a target some distance ahead of the primary one. Such a raid would have all the trappings of a full-scale assault. The Mosquitos would mark the target with illuminators and indicators, and these flares would be centred on by other Mosquitos while a small force of supporting four-engined bombers would come in and bomb. It was a tactic so convincing that the German controllers were usually tricked into believing that it was the start of a major raid and sending in their night-fighters. The ten minutes or so that it took the fighters to get to the scene, plus the ten-minute flight back to their base, was often all that was necessary to get the main force over the real target and away again.

It was Pathfinder Bennett's contention that group commanders very often did not fully appreciate why P.F.F. Headquarters made provision for such dog-legs in their routes. In a personal conversation about the Nuremberg raid, he said, "I opposed the long straight route because clearly the conditions were far too dangerous for such a tactic – particularly when we had been warned that there was a strong chance of there being bright moonlight. Nuremberg turned out to be a very expensive raid. I believe it would still have involved high losses, even with our proposed route; but certainly they would not have been so high as those which were incurred. The wind that night lost us many aircraft through them being blown over heavily defended flak belts, where they became the targets for concentrated and accurate box-barrages.

"The good navigators discovered the true speed of the wind and accordingly corrected their courses. The bad navigators did not, and the result was that the main force

–instead of being a compact and narrow stream – was spread out to a depth of about fifty miles, and this made interception of them by the fighters easier.

"The dog-legging and the dummies we had proposed would have added about two per cent to the flying distance and the time in the air. That is not much – just a few minutes: and I believe this would have fooled most if not all of the German night-fighting force."

Furthermore, Bennett does not believe that there would have been any serious risk of the bombers coming back as dawn was breaking. The little extra time that would have been added to their flight through jinking would not, he thinks, have incurred the risk of them having to operate in partial daylight.

He says of the Pathfinders' diversionary tactics, "Efforts to confuse the enemy and throw off his defensive measures had met with varying success – from one hundred per cent downwards: but these efforts never completely failed. In fact, I would claim that these tactics were one of the greatest contributions the P.F.F. made in the bomber offensive. The bright night of the Nuremberg operation made spoof targets and complex routing even more essential."

And he totally disagrees with assertions made at the time that the action was a catastrophic accident that occurred by chance. It was caused, he says, and was not merely accidental. Indeed, with outspoken frankness, he states that one of the few things with which he agreed in the official history of the air offensive against Germany was the finding that the operational planning of the raid was "uncharacteristically bad and unimaginative".

This, of course, is a view diametrically opposed to that of Sir Ralph Cochrane. But Bennett is not unsupported in his contention. The two Pathfinder leaders on the raid, Wing Commander Daniels and Squadron Leader Creswell, second it.

"I heard at the time, and have always believed, that

Bennett refused to send his force on such a hare-brained route," says Creswell, adding, "but he was overruled by the A.O.C.'s conference. He submitted to their ruling with the remark 'The blood is on their heads'. This was in character for him."

Chapter Twenty-one

Bomber-crew fatalities resulting from the Nuremberg raid totalled nearly ten times the number suffered by the Germans, including those caused by bombs dropped on Schweinfurt and Bamberg by stray aircraft.

A report compiled immediately after the raid by the Luftgaukommando VII (the air district covering the Nuremberg area) War Diary gave the German losses as follows:

Killed: 133

Injured: 412

Homes destroyed: 198

Homes severely damaged: 420

Homes medium damaged: 879

Homes slightly damaged: 2505

Homeless: 2400

Fires started: 120 large, 65 medium and 420 small.

Industrial undertakings: Large fire started at the works of Gebr. Decker. Railway lines to Regensburg, Eger and Amberg temporarily cut. Major damage inflicted on the Neumayr Rolling Mills, Viktoria, and the United Margarine Works.

Bombs dropped: 30 mines; 1450 H.E. (11 duds); 52,000 incendiary bombs and 8000 phosphorous bombs. 6 mines, 110 H.E. and numerous incendiary bombs dropped on several decoy sites.

The Nuremberg Office for War Damage, however – in an investigation confined solely to the effects of the raid on the city itself – found that the casualties were very much lower when separated from those of nearby Schweinfurt and Bamberg. Its report gave these figures.

Dead: Men – 28; Women – 24; Children – 8.

Foreigners: 14 men and 1 woman.

Of this total of 75, 37 were buried by rubble, 19 killed outright and 19 burnt to death.

Homes destroyed: 139; homes severely damaged – 238; homes moderately damaged – 956; homes slightly damaged – 2586.

Industrial and commercial buildings: Totally destroyed – 23; severely damaged – 26; moderately damaged – 47; slightly damaged – 110.

Public buildings: Totally destroyed – 6; severely damaged – 19; moderately damaged – 26; slightly damaged – 26.

Other buildings: Destroyed – 84; severely damaged – 42; moderately damaged – 40; slightly damaged – 124.

The War Damage Office, when it had had time to make a more thorough analysis of the raid, put the number of homeless at 11,000. And it listed the main areas of damage in the city as Buchenbühl, Kesselerstrasse, Frühere SS-Kaserne (former SS barracks), Kongresshalle and König-strasse. Its estimate of the number of bombs dropped on Nuremberg was: Mines – 18; H.E. – 850; Incendiary – 28,000; and Phosphorous – 5000.

Nuremberg was indeed fortunate to have been spared the full fury of a saturation attack.

What may have impressed itself on the Germans was the proportion of incendiary bombs carried by their enemy in relation to bombs of other types. The explanation for that was that the British Air Staff had for some time regarded fire bombs as the best weapon for attacking cities – a view that was not shared by Harris, who had deep faith in high-explosive bombs with light cases to give the greatest blast effect. His force had at its disposal 4000lb and 8000lb high-capacity bombs; but although he argued that high-explosive bombs had a more damaging effect on the morale of civilians, the Air Staff insisted that unless circumstances decreed otherwise a bomb-load should be in the ratio of two-thirds incendiaries to one-third high-explosives.

The Air Staff's overriding decision on this was influenced by an investigation, the result of which had shown that whereas every ton of 8000lb high-explosive bombs dropped destroyed or damaged, on average, nearly two acres of built-up area, and the same weight of 4000lb high-explosive bombs a little less, each ton of fire-bombs devastated three and a quarter acres. An example was the thousand-bomber raid on Cologne in 1942 – for which Harris had had to throw in well over three hundred aircraft from training groups to make up the number. One thousand four hundred and fifty-five tons of bombs had been dropped, nearly two-thirds of them incendiaries. More than six hundred acres of the city's built-up area had been completely destroyed, the incendiaries had caused some twelve thousand fires – two thousand five hundred of them major outbreaks – and the death-roll had totalled four hundred and eighty-six.

The citizens of Nuremberg therefore had reason to be grateful for the doggedness with which the night-fighters had repeatedly pressed home their attacks on the bombers, thus saving them from the fate that had overtaken Cologne, Berlin, Essen and other towns which had been pounded into rubble by the merciless area-bombing of Harris's heavies. Frightful as the raid had seemed to them at its height, when they had crept from their shelters after the all-clear sirens had sounded they had been surprised to find less damage than they had expected: although the eleven thousand homeless among them were a confirmation of the determination with which the bomber crews had persevered with their attack despite the relentless efforts made by the night-fighters to beat them back.

Nevertheless, it was a fact that Nuremberg had got off comparatively lightly; and it was no surprise to the people of the city when a communiqué was issued announcing that the German air forces had achieved their greatest victory and that the British had suffered their greatest-ever losses. In fact, to commemorate the occasion, Goering had sent a personal telegram congratulating the night-fighter-crews with a special mention for those in the 1st Jagdkorps.

And the Luftwaffe had cause to feel elated over the night's work. Night-fighter casualties had been infinitesimal compared with those of Bomber Command – for of the two hundred and forty-six single-engined and twin-engined aircraft engaged in the action only five had been lost, whereas the Command Centre of the Air Defence of Germany claimed that one hundred and seven bombers had been shot down for certain, with another six probably destroyed.

The 1st Jagdkorps listed its losses as:

1st Jagddivision: Aircrew – 1 killed, 4 missing.
                   Aircraft – 2 missing, 3 damaged and 1 with over 60 per cent damage.

2nd Jagddivision: Aircrew – 2 missing.
                   Aircraft – 2 missing and 1 with over 60 per cent damage.

3rd Jagddivision: Aircrew – 2 killed, 2 missing and 1 wounded.
                   Aircraft – 1 missing and 3 with damage over 60 per cent.

This report ended with a special note: "Oberleutnant Becker, Staffelkapitan in Night-Fighter Squadron 1, shot down 7 British bombers during the night of 30th/31st March."

The battle-report singled out the 1st Fighter Corps for special mention and listed the grounds for their success as: early detection of the bomber stream and its subsequent moves after it left its bases; the take-off of all the twin-engined fighters at the time that the outward-flying bombers had set course towards the middle of the western frontier of the Reich; the flight of the bombers over the Rhein-Main area, which took them into the heart of the German night-fighter network, thus allowing all the twin-engined fighters to go into action in good time and well within their operating range; the use of the new air-borne radar apparatus SN2, which could not be seriously jammed in the course of the night-pursuit operation; good flying visibility and moonlight, which enabled the fighters to visually identify the bombers at about 1000 metres; the early shoot-downs of bombers in the Lüttich-Bonn-Koblenz area, which lit up the scene and helped the night-fighters to locate the stream; the long period provided for the fighters to pursue the bombers because the hunt had begun in the area left of the Rhine; the extraordinary coincidence that the radio-beacons Ida and Otto, which had been used as assembly points for the twin-engined fighters, were flown over by the bomber stream.

The German Air Defence chiefs found that the single-engined night-fighters had been less successful than the twin-engined ones because they had not been brought into action over the target area: but then, the single-engined fighters had been unable to follow the bombers because they had no airborne radar with which to vector them. Their operations had also been hindered by the fact that they had been held back for some time as a precaution against the bombers attacking Frankfurt-am-Main or swinging on to some other target in central Germany, particularly Berlin.

Pathfinder Bennett's contention that P.F.F. diversionary tactics confused the enemy and never completely failed found confirmation in the German battle-analysis, which stated that the decoy operations of the Mosquitos prevented the ground controllers from making an earlier judgment of the probable targets to be attacked. It went on to comment: "The Headquarters Command of the 1st Fighter Corps was comparatively late in coming to the conclusion that the British attack was aimed at Nuremberg: Because of the German counter-attack, the confused British bomber force came over Nuremberg only gradually and took a comparatively long time to launch the attack. In consequence, the command of the Corps assumed for some time that the real attack would be launched on some other target. During this period of uncertainty about the battle situation, the single-engined fighters had exhausted their fuel."

It is easy, with hindsight, to argue that the ultimate goal of the bombers should have been recognised sooner: but in fact, it is remarkable that the controllers were able to vector the fighters into the path of the lead bombers as early as they did. With Harris's bomber force liable to swing off to attack any of a dozen places at any time during its nearly two-hundred-and-fifty-miles-long flight from Charleroi to Fulda, the controllers could hardly be blamed for the caution they showed before finally deciding on the true objective.

Oberst im Generalstab Janke, who was then deputy commander and chief of staff of the 7th Fighter Division and later its commanding officer, was full of praise for the supreme command position in rightly forecasting that the raid would be in the region of southern Germany. In a detailed personal communication, Janke – who now lives in Munich – makes it clear that the British bomber force was subjected to dispositions and tactical decisions which were all in favour of the defences. He listed the main ones as: the especially favourable weather conditions for night interceptions; the concentrated assembly of fighters from bases in the rearward areas of Germany, and particularly the concentration over radio-beacon Ida; the flight of the bombers – conveniently for the Germans – through the 'Himmelbett' ground-to-air radar boxes of the No. 5 Fighter Division in Belgium and Holland, which presented the German air defences with good opportunities to attack early in the inward flight of the bombers and allowed them to sluice in Nos. 1, 4 and 5 Night Fighter Squadrons until they were later taken under the direction of the 7th Division; the well-filtered and accurate air-situation reports of the 7th Division that enabled the controllers to transmit continuous and precise reports of the altitude, size, depth and estimated length of the bomber stream to the night-fighter pilots; the prompt and accurate spotting of the few decoys, course changes and diversionary tactics used by the bombers.

But the crucial factor was that the ground controllers had eventually recognised, in good time and with near certainty, that the main attack would be on Nuremberg.

Explains Janke, "All the required factors came into play, so that the outcome and the success of the German night force in the command area of the 7th Division was only a logical consequence and the product of a first-rate piece of co-operation and co-ordination.

"No one can be singled out as being directly responsible for this defence victory. It was excellent teamwork in which all units on the ground and in the air pulled their full weight. The hard training work in the radar stations, in the night-fighter squadrons and in Divisional H.Q. had been crowned with success. This was not always easy, for we had to be perpetually on guard against the posting of aircraft-reporting officers and subordinate personnel from their district observation areas [radar stations] or from divisional headquarters once they were trained in their jobs.

"At the end of every enemy air operation we would hold a central de-briefing over a telephone link-up, and this would be the time when we discussed what mistakes we had made, what new knowledge of the enemy we had gained and what new methods were needed. This helped to add to the already intensive study we had made of Bomber Command and its methods.

"There would also be a central telephone de-briefing with the commanders, group-leaders and individual successful night-fighter pilots after an action, and we gained much by this.

"The radar search equipment we used in our night-fighters was by now very efficient, and with it young and inexperienced crews – up to the strength of about four aircraft – could be directed into the bomber stream by older and more experienced night-fighter crews. This equipment was used with much success by No. 6 Night-Fighter Squadron during the Nuremberg raid.

"In the extension, improvement and security of the ground-to-ground and ground-to-air control communications the 7th Division had very advanced techniques because they had built and installed VHF R/T transmitter-receivers for plain language communications at Pfaffen, so that in the event of the telephone system breaking down important orders could be sent by VHF."

Courage, skill and youth were the basic requirements for both bomber and night-fighter crews. But the night-fighter commanders, who pitted their wits almost nightly against Bomber Command, were another breed. They had to have something more. On their judgments, their assessments, their decisions hung not only the lives of their aircrews but also those of the civilian population of the cities and towns they were committed to protect.

"Besides 'soldier's luck'," says Janke, "which, for all that might be said about military skill and special scientific knowledge, every responsible commander must have – especially in a battle involving combined forces – the night-fighter commander needs something else. He must also rely upon an intuitive, intellectual perception. It is a faculty that one is born with and cannot learn, giving one the ability to 'live' in the element of the air, to react swiftly, alone and correctly, when confronted with unpredictable events in the three-dimensional battle space. We often went for a week without more than one or two hours' sleep – for no sooner was the night activity over than the American daylight bombers came roaring in from Italy and England to add to the spiritual and mental strain under which we worked. It was work that never really ended."

Of those long, difficult nights when the bombs rained down on Germany, Janke comments, "Both sides only did their duty, although they fought under different flags.

The esteem in which one holds a fair opponent should have first place. In my view, the former German Luftwaffe consistently followed this principle to the bitter end in their battle against a more powerful opponent."

This assertion was borne out by many former night-fighter crews who, in personal communications, stressed that they had not been actuated by hate when going into action against the bombers. And there is certainly no recorded instance of a night-fighter gunning down any British airman who had baled out.

Hans Meissner of Karlsruhe, then a Leutnant but now a Major in the German Air Force, wrote, "My duty was done when the attacked aircraft went down. The object was not to kill the crew but to destroy engines and tanks. Thus I can say that with the exception of my first kills, when I was rather nervous, large numbers of the bombers' crews always succeeded in descending by parachute. I do not mention this in order to extenuate or glorify. It was a bare fact. Our conversations prior to an action and afterwards were sober, without boasting. Even today there is not much to say. All of us, friends or adversaries, had at least one thing in common – death, which might have taken any of us at any time."

Meissner could well have been excused had he thirsted for revenge on the bomber crews, for in an attack on Berlin he lost a close relative. "But," he says, "the same happened to many of my comrades; and every one of us worried about the lives of our relatives after attacks on our cities."

Officially credited with shooting down twenty-one four-engined bombers, two of them during the Nuremberg raid, Meissner pays this tribute to the bomber crews:

"My experiences of air fights, and the reports of my comrades, revealed that the British airmen were outstanding fighters. It happened many times that we got return fire even from aircraft going down ablaze. In the briefings after actions the brave attitude of the adversary was stressed – and the losses that the bombers and their night-fighters inflicted on us proved it. I had the opportunity only once to talk to a shot-down crew. Their attitude remained upright and sincere. Our conversation then became comradely, the enmity was forgotten. My adversaries did nothing else but their duty and had relatives at home who worried about them as I had relatives who worried about me.'

A pilot who downed four bombers at Nuremberg, Leutnant Wilhelm Seuss, writes, "Please allow me also to mention the great bravery of the crews of the British bombers who carried out their operation with astonishing calm, just as though there had been no German fighter opposition. Even though there may now be some public and sceptical criticism of Bomber Command's attacks on German cities, one should not include the crews of the aircraft in those criticisms."

Of the tactics of the bombers that attacked Nuremberg, Seuss says, "The high losses were mostly due to a misinterpretation by the British of the weather conditions that prevailed at the time. Feints of the formations which raided Nuremberg would not have given them any help. But a feinted attack to any other target in northern Germany would have diminished the night-fighter force against the bombers raiding Nuremberg. There was a feint, but only a small one, over the North Sea – but the formation did not cross the coast and it was recognised as a feint, so the night-fighter wings in northern Germany were ordered to the south."

Hauptmann Fritz Lau, credited with shooting down a Halifax during the raid, also had respect for the bomber crews. A month after Nuremberg, he downed a British aircraft over the French coast. Of this he says, "I saw one of the crew bale out over the Channel and I believed it to be my absolute duty to worry about his fate, so I notified the rescue service through my station headquarters immediately after I landed. I gave the rescue service the position and time of the shoot-down so that they could get the search and rescue operation under way as quickly as possible."

"There was no feeling of hate against the bomber crews," writes Erich Handke of Dortmund, who was an Oberfeldwebel and radar operator to night-fighter ace Martin Drewes. "We knew that they also believed they were doing their duty. Our whole ambition was to get as many bombers down as quickly as possible so as to save the lives of civilians and prevent those senseless destructions." He also recalls that after their high losses at Nuremberg the bombers gave the night-fighters a three-week respite before their next raid – which was in bad weather with no moonlight.

It was a much needed respite, for the strain of continuous night-flying was felt just as intensely by the interceptors as it was by the bomber crews. Oberleutnant Helmuth Schulte of Opladen, who shot down four bombers at Nuremberg, sums up what it was like in this way: "Enjoyable? No, night-fighting was not. It was a most bitter experience that broke many nerves and had few survivors. We had to withstand much anxiety. This was due less to the fighting itself, which took place in the dark and in which we had the better chance, than to the need to fly in bad weather in conditions under which normally no man would set foot in an aircraft.

"Night-fighting in anger, inspired by a feeling of hate or because a comrade had been killed in a bombing raid, was not possible. In order to have any success and to stay alive it was essential that experience and concentration should be the first qualities in the flying, though it is true that the swashbuckling touch was often necessary as well.

"What was most important was to find the in-flying bomber stream – and in this the carefully-worked-out flight plan was vital. But very often it could only be worked out after take-off, and even then it had to be altered. Also the business of getting the bomber into one's sights was often tedious. We sat well down under the bomber and then climbed slowly until we were within fifty to a hundred metres of it. Then I lined up and aimed between the two starboard engines. At the instant that I fired I would bank away to the left. Thus all the shots went from below into the fuel tanks of the bomber, which usually burst into flames immediately.

"Because we usually came from low down and from astern, we were rarely spotted by the British air-gunners and attracted no defensive fire. Being lower than the bomber, we could keep with it and observe it against the background of the night sky. If we managed to catch the head of the bomber stream, we used to hold back in order to more easily shoot down the waves of aircraft following.

"Before the Nuremberg raid there had been an easing off in the British long-range night-fighter attacks on our aerodromes. These attacks were often unpleasant and brought us many losses, but they were not decisive. This was because usually bad weather prevailed and this went against the long-distance night-fighters. But after the Nuremberg raid the bombers, when they eventually came back, were protected by these long-range fighters which caused us very heavy losses. Above all, we could hardly ever fly on a direct course without running into the danger of being caught by a long-range British night-fighter.

"Night-fighting was nerve-racking; and the few who survived it had, above all things, flying skill and occasional luck."

So it was with the bomber crews too. Their nerves also cracked sometimes. And one would have expected this to be readily understood. Regrettably, though, it was not – at least, not by the chairborne top brass, in whose incredibly inept estimation nerve-shattered airmen were cowards. Not that they would come out with the direct accusation. They had to coin a new phrase for it – "lack of moral fibre", which in turn was abbreviated to "L.M.F." And those three letters were about the best-kept secret of the war – until the whole thing was exposed in the book *Maximum Effort*.*

* By the author of this book.

To be tagged L.M.F. was to be proclaimed a coward. It was as simple as that. And the stigma held more terror for many men than the living nightmare of the raids that had brought them to the point of nervous exhaustion. For fear of being branded L.M.F. too many airmen carried on with their flying duties when they were in no mental condition to face another operation – some of them, numbed and without hope, going silently to certain death. Such was the malevolent power of that damning and viciously unfair phrase.

Airmen who couldn't hide their mental state were posted within hours, in case they affected others. No one was told that they were going and no one was told where they were sent – but the grapevine eventually carried every detail back to the operational squadrons. And so it was known that sergeants, flight sergeants and warrant officers were stripped of their rank and their wings and were given the most degrading of menial tasks at the worst bases. Furthermore – to complete their punishment for having the failings of ordinary human beings – they had to wear their old uniforms, which showed clearly where their rank and wings had been and assured them the embarrassment of having to explain why they had been stripped.

Outside of the service, however, the R.A.F. went to extraordinary pains to keep L.M.F. a top secret – a high-level decision actuated by the belief that the nation's morale might be adversely affected if it became generally known that some of the 'intrepid, infallible' flyers of Bomber Command had cracked-up under the strain of unimaginable hazards. So men who had been through hell and had now reached the limit of their resources were privately pilloried – made to fear the scorn of their comrades if they succumbed to their nerves; made to dread being called 'chicken'.

What was it, anyway, that kept these men going? What breed of man was it that could come through an inferno like the Nuremberg raid with the knowledge that he'd be taking similar risks perhaps only a night or so later?

Certainly there was no cloak of blissful ignorance about the odds. One man in three was killed in Bomber Command. This was a statistic, and no member of a bomber crew needed to be a brilliant mathematician to work it out for himself. The airmen knew what it was all about; and once the effects of the pep-pills with which they had been issued had worn off, reality came flooding back. They would awaken with raw nerves to live again the raid they had just been on; and with the memory of it fresh they would dread the next one. Their battle-fatigued minds would fill with thoughts of throwing it in now – before it was too late. Common sense would tell them that with each additional operation they were tempting Providence: the dice were loaded against them. But what was the alternative? To be classed L.M.F. To be sneered at and scorned as a coward by comrades whose friendship and respect mattered. For the many, it was no choice at all.

There were seldom any L.M.F. cases after a crew's first trip – understandably. New crews were usually so bewildered and bemused that they did not fully realise what they had just been through. But by their fifth trip they knew, and the horror of it lanced them. In most cases, however, they steeled themselves and carried on.

It was such an individual thing. An airman with more than half a tour of operations behind him might suddenly know in his heart that he could never complete the required thirty and therefore throw in the towel. His past record would count for nothing. Just like a novice, the veteran would be branded L.M.F. and hurried into humiliation – indelibly marked with those crucifying letters.

But bomber crews never talked about L.M.F. among themselves, for no one knew who might be the next to have a nervous breakdown.

Air Vice-Marshal Bennett, who unlike the majority of the R.A.F.'s high-ranking officers had flown in action in World War 2 (he was shot down over Norway and escaped), understood the battle-fatigue of bomber aircrews and said this of them in his book *Pathfinder*:

> When one appreciates that each such raid was generally as dangerous as a major battle on land or sea, one gets something of an idea of the sacrifice made by some bomber crews.

He went on to record that in his opinion the contribution of an aircrew member of Bomber Command who completed an operational tour, or who died in the process, was far greater than that of any other fighting man – R.A.F., Navy or Army. And he added:

> The contribution of a Pathfinder, in the same terms of intensity and duration of danger – and indeed responsibility – was at least twice that of other Bomber Command crews. Great Britain and the Empire have, in the goodly time of ten years since the end of the war, strangely failed to erect any Nelson's column in memory of Bomber Command, the most powerful striking force in all British history.

In contrast, Herr Janke points out that on the memorial erected at Geisenheim-Rhein to the German Union of Fighter Flyers there is the following inscription:

> To the dead fighter flyers of all nations.

Chapter Twenty-two

Not only did the catastrophic losses sustained by Bomber Command on Nuremberg earn for the inhabitants of Germany's big cities a fairly long respite from nightly mass-saturation air attacks, but it also led to a drastic alteration in the entire strategy of the R.A.F.'s deep-penetration policy.

For nearly a month the prime-target towns of Germany benefited from a lull in major air attacks. "It was" – as Churchill recorded in his history of the war – "proof of the power which the enemy's night-fighter force, strengthened by the best crews from other vital fronts, had developed under our relentless offensive."

Official historians also conceded that the performance of the German night-fighter force at Nuremberg was more than just a flash in the pan. "It was generally held," they wrote, "and particularly so by the C-in-C Bomber Command, that the outcome endangered the future prospect of sustained and massive long-range operations at least in the absence of radical remedial action."

The prospect of massive raids deep into Germany by any route became dismally bleak and remained so until the battle for France neared its end. There was only one large-scale raid of any note, and that was really in the nature of an experiment to test a new method of marking a target from a low altitude. The experiment – which was to have far-reaching effects on future bombing strategy – was carried out by Cochrane's No. 5 Group in a raid on Munich on the night of 24th/25th April 1944 with, at the same time, a diversionary attack on Karlsruhe by Halifaxes of No. 4 Group.

Group Captain Leonard Cheshire, who was then Wing Commander of No. 617 Squadron, carried out the low-level marking in a Mosquito. Because the weather was so bad that night he had had to take a route that brought him under heavy fire from the Augsburg ground-guns: and from then on, until reaching Munich, he had been under constant fire.

Over Munich, coned by searchlights, he had to dive to seven hundred feet to release the new-type flares. Then, to draw the attention of other Bomber Command aircraft to the flares, he circuited the city at one thousand feet, his Mosquito being repeatedly hit by flak but not downed. (Cheshire, who had already completed four tours of operations, was awarded the Victoria Cross for this and other equally courageous exploits.)

Apart from this operation, however, the bomber offensive was switched almost immediately to the more lightly defended targets in France. Indeed, it was just as well that – as had been previously arranged – Bomber Command was placed under the control of the Supreme Commander during the months before and after the invasion. For in any event, the unquestionable ascendancy that the German night-fighter force had so clearly demonstrated in the defence of Nuremberg, coupled with the shorter hours of darkness, would have vetoed any plans for the resumption of area attacks on the Third Reich. The big raids, which had begun in the spring of 1943, therefore came to a temporary halt in April 1944. And what had they achieved?

Harris has stated that up to the end of October 1943, 167,230 tons of bombs had been dropped on thirty-eight principal German towns; and he has claimed that they destroyed 20,991 acres – or about a quarter of the area attacked.

At first sight these figures seem impressive; but on closer

analysis the bomber chief's claims appear to be not so conclusive. The official historians of the Royal Air Force, in Volume III of their work, comment:

> Harris had made his attacks not so much in accordance with the Combined Bomber Offensive Plan, laid down soon after the Casablanca Conference, as in an effort to follow out a plan by which those German cities containing the largest population were assaulted. The 38 towns which he had bombed contained 72 per cent of the urban population of Germany, but this was less then 33 per cent of the total population and amounted to no more than 25 million souls. Even if the built-up area destroyed in each town was to reach 50 per cent – whereas by the end of 1943 it was about 25 per cent – the enemy would still be able to carry on the fight. The Combined Operational Planning Committee accordingly urged that to concentrate on towns containing vital industrial objectives was the more effective strategy.

But whether or not Bomber Command's strategy was effective, its cost in aircraft and crews was heavy. Losses at the start of the offensive were in the region of 3·6 per cent, but they rose sharply until July 1943 – when the introduction of 'window' was responsible for a decrease. During the whole of this period, Bomber Command carried out more than 74,900 sorties and lost 2824 aircraft, with the number of aircrew killed or missing being in excess of 20,000.

There had been three main problems confronting the planners of the bomber offensive at the outset. The first was the need for a sufficient number of airfields big enough to take four-engined Lancasters and Halifaxes, a sufficient number of aircraft to put on the fields, and the crews to man them. Secondly, the aircraft needed to be fitted with radar devices to help them through bad weather conditions. And thirdly, means had to be found to thwart the enemy's defences.

By the end of 1943 the first requirement had been partially met; and the second was largely fulfilled by the introduction of Gee, Oboe and H2S. But the third, and perhaps the most vital, was never effectively resolved – as Nuremberg had so disastrously proved.

When it did eventually resume its area bombing of Germany, therefore, Bomber Command introduced new timing tactics based primarily on up-to-the minute wind calculations in an attempt to minimise its losses. The procedure was that the best navigators in an operational force worked out the prevailing wind-speeds and wind-directions as they experienced them and transmitted their findings back to England. There they were analysed, and their mean average was in turn broadcast to every aircraft in the bomber force – thus ensuring that all navigated on common calculations and so kept the concentration tight. If after the start of the operation the winds varied greatly from those forecast at briefing, the time on the target could be either put back or brought forward during the flight so as to maintain accurate timing and conserve fuel. In addition, much of the target marking was to be done by low-level Mosquitos under the supervision of a master-bomber. And elaborate diversionary attacks were to be included in all flight plans.

To further overcome the weather difficulties, and to lessen the odds on fighter interception, almost every bomber was equipped with H2S and a fighter-approach warning device such as Fishpond – the efficiency of which had been amply demonstrated during the Nuremberg action.

Ironically, all of this came about at the very time that the Luftwaffe's day-fighters relinquished control of the skies above Germany.

In a reassessment of the Nuremberg operation, in personal conversation, Sir Arthur Harris expressed the opinion that in the prevailing weather conditions on that night the losses would have been about the same regardless of the route taken: but if he'd had an accurate weather forecast before him on the day of the raid it is doubtful that he would have gone ahead with the operation. Harris, however, is not the type of man to shift the blame entirely on to the shoulders of the R.A.F. Met men – who, he stressed, were working under the tremendous handicap of being denied essential weather data from large tracts of western Europe and other important sources.

Far from maligning the meteorological department, Harris believes that but for its basic information Bomber Command's casualty rate might have been twice as high as it was. He had been keenly aware that day of the gnawing anxieties besetting the Met men as to whether or not they had made the right predictions; and so, to allay their fears to some extent, he had instituted a conference over the 'scrambler' telephone with the senior Met officers in each bomber group. And then, because there was still uncertainty, he had done what he normally did in such circumstances – he made the final decision himself.

Like Cochrane, he vehemently disagrees with the official historians' finding that the planning of the Nuremberg operation was – to quote their words again – "uncharacteristically bad and unimaginative"; and he explains, "There was not an endless supply of tactics that could have been used, and to have thought out new ones over a period of three years and over a thousand raids naturally limited them. Some were bound not to be too successful. In sending the force in one stream to Nuremberg we thought we would fool the German night-controller, who we considered would not believe it. We had used in the past so many tactics and diversions – making out that such-and-such a city was to be the target and then heading for the real one – that we hoped the straight run to Nuremberg would fox the Germans into thinking that we would, as in the past, suddenly turn off before the city was reached and deliver our attack elsewhere . . . And in flying over two German night-fighter bases, the bombers may well have avoided a dozen such bases."

Of the group commanders' objections to Pathfinder

Bennett's route, Harris declared, "It was often the case that a group commander was in the minority opinion, but the final decision was a majority one. We always got the opinions of the main-force group commanders and we encouraged them to criticise any routes either to myself or to Saundby. The route to Nuremberg was drawn up after the usual for-and-against discussions which took place with the group commanders.

"We were always astonished that there was not more than one Nuremberg, for over the years you cannot expect to hit the jackpot all the time – and similarly, you could not prevent the enemy from hitting it. The Nuremberg casualties were indeed high, but my reaction was that we had been expecting something like this to happen ever since we started the big penetration raids; and I consider we were lucky that it had not reached this proportion more often.

"The answer to the Nuremberg action is that the casualties should not be looked on as those of just one battle but should be spaced over the whole period of the bomber offensive."

Harris, who had always been anxious to find ways of cutting his bomber losses, had frequently tried to get long-range fighter support for his force – but without success. After the lesson of Nuremberg, however, the Mosquito Light Night Striking Force was expanded and given the onerous job of flying among the bombers to seek out the German night-fighters. And a risky assignment it turned out to be – for many of the bomber gunners fired on any twin-engined aircraft they happened to see, on the maxim that it was better to be sorry than dead.

On the other hand, many Mosquito pilots reported that they had been able to steal up on a bomber, completely unseen and unsuspected by the gunners, and could easily have shot it down – thus confirming that visibility from the bomber turrets was extremely limited. German night-fighter pilots had, of course, discovered this for themselves and naturally enough made their attacks from the blind spot below and to either side of a bomber, their long-range machine-guns and cannon enabling them to stay beyond the range of the bomber's .303 Brownings while they pumped fire into it at will. A belly turret like that in the American Flying Fortress would have saved a great many bombers from destruction: but Harris's pleas for a more formidable type of turret had always been fobbed off in the same way as his argument for fighter protection at night.

Of his futile attempts to get fighter protection before Nuremberg, Harris said, "The excuse was that we had no long-range fighters. But we could have had them had the decision been taken in time. The American Mustang, which was the finest long-range fighter of the war, was originally turned down flat by the Americans who produced it. This was reported to me, when I was in charge of the R.A.F. delegation in Washington, by one of our most brilliant test pilots, Christopher Clarkson, who said it had to be given more power. On that recommendation we took the Mustang and fitted it with Rolls-Royce engines in place of the American Allison engine. But when the Americans came into the war they virtually took over the lot.

"It was a similar story with our turrets. Visibility from them was extremely poor, while the four .303 machine-guns in them were totally inadequate as an effective stopper against the heavy-calibre machine-guns and cannon of the German night-fighters. We should have had at least two .05 heavy machine-guns, as the American bombers had. The armament people at the Air Ministry said at the time that they could produce a .05 turret, so I got on to the famous armaments firm of Roses in Gainsborough. Roses produced for me a working turret which had two .05 guns, and these would have greatly increased the fire power and range of the bomber gunners. We could have had them had the Air Ministry's armaments people put as much energy into getting them as they did into arguing that they could not be produced."

But whether the Lancasters and Halifaxes that took part in the Nuremberg raid would have fared any better with .05 turrets is highly doubtful. At best, they might have sent down a few more night-fighters. But they would have had no effect on the other enemy – the weather. And Harris is the first to admit that on the Nuremberg operation his bombers were also fighting the weather – appalling weather. Which prompted him to remember, "Churchill never interfered with me. He never gave me an order – except one, and that was, 'I do not want you to fight the weather as well as the enemy.' "

Despite this oblique indication from Harris that Churchill was not concerned with Bomber Command's choice of targets, Sir Robert Saundby remained convinced to the end that it was pressure from the wartime Prime Minister that had led to the launching of the catastrophic raid on Nuremberg.

Chapter Twenty-three

"There has been much criticism of Bomber Command and its achievements. I don't give a damn what they say about me, but I do get angry when they try to minimise the great achievements of the bomber aircrews. I am always amazed that anyone survived Bomber Command service."

So says Harris today: and his defence of the men who manned his Lancasters and Halifaxes is to be expected, for no one knows better than he what they faced and what their chances of survival were. Certainly no one had more reason than he to be aware of the fact that during the period from the spring of 1943, when the bomber offensive really began, to the invasion, when it tapered off, very few crews did indeed survive a tour of operations.

In the main, however, it is not the aircrews who come under fire from post-war critics but the bomber offensive itself and the man who directed it. Yet Harris, who was later to become Marshal of the Royal Air Force, was not responsible for the policy of bombing German cities and towns. He will shrug off the charge that his bombing was indiscriminate and inhuman with the tart reminder that all war is inhuman, but the fact remains that the decision to area-bomb Germany had been made and was in force when he took over as Commander-in-Chief of Bomber Command. A directive for the area-bombing of enemy cities and towns was issued by the Air Staff a week before he succeeded Air Marshal Sir Richard Peirse, in February 1942. And its underlying motives were to destroy Germany's capacity and will to carry on the war and to meet in some measure Russia's incessant demands for a Second Front. Bomber